PLAYING THEIR GAMES

Also by Kiki Swinson

The Playing Dirty Series: *Playing Dirty* and *Notorious*
The Candy Shop
A Sticky Situation
The Wifey Series: *Wifey, I'm Still Wifey, Life After Wifey,*
Still Wifey Material
Wife Extraordinaire Series: *Wife Extraordinaire* and *Wife*
Extraordinaire Returns
Cheaper to Keep Her Series: Books 1–5
The Score Series: *The Score* and *The Mark*
Dead on Arrival
The Black Market Series: *The Black Market, The Safe*
House, Property of the State
The Deadline
Public Enemy #1
Playing with Fire

ANTHOLOGIES
Sleeping with the Enemy (with Wahida Clark)
Heist and *Heist 2* (with De'nesha Diamond)
Lifestyles of the Rich and Shameless (with Noire)
A Gangster and a Gentleman (with De'nesha Diamond)
Most Wanted (with Nikki Turner)
Still Candy Shopping (with Amaleka McCall)
Fistful of Benjamins (with De'nesha Diamond)
Schemes and *Dirty Tricks* (with Saundra)
Bad Behavior (with Noire)

Published by Kensington Publishing Corp.

PLAYING THER GAMES

KIKI SWINSON

DAFINA

www.kensingtonbooks.com

DAFINA BOOKS are published by

Kensington Publishing Corp.
119 West 40th Street
New York, NY 10018

All Kensington Titles, Imprints, and Distributed Lines are available at special quantity discounts for bulk purchases for sales promotions, premiums, fund-raising, and educational or institutional use. Special book excerpts or customized printings can also be created to fit specific needs. For details, write or phone the office of the Kensington special sales manager: Kensington Publishing Corp., 119 West 40th Street, New York, NY 10018, attn: Special Sales Department, Phone: 1-800-221-2647.

Library of Congress Card Catalogue Number: 2022931850

The DAFINA logo is a trademark of Kensington Publishing Corp.

ISBN: 978-1-4967-3412-9
First Kensington Hardcover Edition: July 2022

ISBN-13: 978-1-4967-3418-1 (ebook)

10 9 8 7 6 5 4 3 2 1

Printed in the United States of America

PLAYING THEIR GAMES

1

Yoshi

Today marked my sixty-first day working at the law firm. I was officially off my probation period. That meant, full medical benefits, sick leave, and vacation time. The pay sucked, but driving a company car and having full access to one of the firm's black American Express credit cards made up for it.

The law firm was owned and operated by identical twin brothers, Aaron and Noah Weinstein. The Weinstein brothers were some very powerful and well-connected men. They've been practicing law for over thirty years. Their law firm was located a block over from Wall Street. Both men moved in the same manner. They spoke using the same lingo. They laughed the same. Their hair was the same. They arrived to work at the same time. They drank the same type of coffee. They hung out at the same bar after leaving the office. And they loved a great game of chess.

The only way I knew how to tell them apart was when one

wore a black suit, the other would sport a blue suit. In their own unique way, both men had their own sense of humor. At the end of the day, they would tell jokes and see whose was the funniest. Aaron managed to get more of the staff members to laugh at his jokes versus Noah. They were both corny in my eyes, but they signed my paychecks, so I laughed every time they opened their mouths.

"Getting ready for that bar exam?" Noah asked me as he walked casually into the office his paralegal, Jillian Parks, and I shared. Jillian was not only Aaron and Noah's paralegal, she was my supervisor too. At first glance, she looked like a dingy-ass white chick in her late twenties. From what I heard, she'd been working for Noah for a couple of years now and thought she ran things. I, for one, noticed how she bullied the receptionist in the waiting area of the office, and I wouldn't tolerate it if she treated me like that. She was so short and thin, all I would have to do was blow on her and she'd fall down to the floor. That's just how tiny she was.

I smiled. "You know I am," I told him, and then I looked back down at the screen of my computer and pretended to be working hard on a deposition Jillian had me recording in a file for a client Noah was representing in a sexual harassment case.

"Have you spoken to Bill yet?" Noah asked Jillian as he stood before her desk.

"Yes, I just spoke with him right before you walked in here," she replied. But I knew she was lying. I'd been at my desk for the past hour and she hadn't talked to anyone on the phone. But she knew that if she told him that she hadn't called his client Bill, he'd chew her ass up and spit her out.

Bill Stanley was one of Noah's millionaire clients. He was the founder and CEO of an investment firm in Manhattan. Bill was currently being sued by a former female employee. Bill wanted this suit to go away, as quickly and quietly as possible. If this suit went to trial, this would ruin his reputation and perhaps bankrupt him. More important, it would put him behind bars for a long time. This would put a stain on Noah's acquittal rate too, and he wouldn't have that. Not in this lifetime.

"Has Mary from the U.S. Attorney's Office gotten back to you with a date?" Noah's questions continued.

"No, she hasn't. But if I don't hear back from her by three, I will call her," Jillian assured him.

"Sounds good," he said, and then he turned around to leave. As he was exiting the office, my boyfriend, Troy, walked by. Troy looked in our direction, but when he saw Noah leaving our office, he tried to turn his head back around to avoid eye contact. That didn't stop Noah from calling his name though. "Hey, Troy," Noah called.

Troy stopped in front of the doorway. "Yes, sir," he said.

"You're just the man that I want to see," he replied as he walked toward him. "Follow me to my office," Noah instructed him, and then he led the way.

I could see the look in Troy's eyes; he wanted to kick himself in the ass for running into Noah. He knew Noah better than everyone in the firm, except for Aaron. Troy was a preppy white guy. He was also a junior partner, and because of it, Noah expected a lot from Troy. Troy basically handled all of Noah's dirty work. He and I had been dating for a month, and one night not too long ago, he and I got drunk at his apartment and he slipped up and told me that Noah used him to pay off witnesses that were involved in his client's court cases. He even had a hand in some jury tampering too. After he realized what he had told me, he begged me not to say a word about it to anyone. I promised him that I wouldn't utter a word. Not even to my parents, since they knew Noah and Aaron on a personal level and were the reason why I got the job hookup in the first place.

"Are you almost done with that deposition?" Jillian asked me.

"Almost," I told her.

"How much longer?"

"Maybe another ten minutes."

"Okay, well, hurry up," she instructed me.

I looked up from my computer and looked over at her. "Are you all right?" I asked nonchalantly. But I was really trying to be sarcastic. But the bitch ignored me, grabbed her telephone, and made a phone call, while I waited for her to answer me. I swear, I had so many names formulated in my head that I'd rather say verbally, but I kept my mouth closed. The word *bitch* wouldn't have been the first name that came out of my mouth.

"Hi, is this Bill?" she started asking through the receiver. I guess she was trying to cover her fucking tracks before Noah got a chance to talk to Bill and found out that she hadn't talked to him, when she told him she did. I knew that she was a bona fide liar, and that she was someone I needed to keep an eye on. The shit I went through back in Virginia while I was in college molded me into a renegade, but I made it so that you wouldn't see it on the surface. I was calculating, and that was my strong suit.

"Noah wanted me to remind you about tonight's meeting at the lounge on Eighth Avenue," she said, and then paused. "Okay, great. And don't forget to bring the new documents you were served yesterday." She continued to talk and then she fell silent again. "Sure, I will let him know."

Immediately after Jillian ended the call, she got up from her desk and left the office. Normally, she'd tell me if anyone was looking for her that she was taking a bathroom break or getting coffee, but she didn't open her mouth.

"Fucking bitch," I mumbled.

She stopped in midstep and looked back at me like she had heard me. "Say something?" she asked.

"I was talking to myself." I lied and gave her a sly smirk.

She rolled her eyes and exited the office.

A few seconds later, Troy come strolling into my office. He looked east and west before he stepped over the threshold. "Hey, baby," he whispered as he rushed over toward my desk. As soon as he came within two feet of me, he leaned in to kiss me on the lips.

After our lips connected, I pushed him back a little. "You know better. What if Jillian would've walked in here and saw us kiss?" I said nervously.

"I saw her go into the bathroom, so she'll be a minute," Troy told me, hoping to calm me down.

"What did Noah want?" I changed the subject.

"He wants me to tag along with him when he meets up with his client Bill."

"But tonight was supposed to be our night. We planned to get Chinese and rent a movie."

"I know, baby. But Noah sprang this on me at the last moment. And I couldn't say no. He's my boss," Troy tried to explain.

"Just admit that you're afraid of him," I teased.

"Come on now. You can't be serious."

"Well, you better man up and act like it," I teased once again.

"So, how's your day going so far?" He changed the subject.

"Jillian is being a bitch today, trying to boss me around. But other than that, it's just a workday for me. What about you?"

"Everything's good."

"Well, why did I see you trying to avoid Noah when you walked by a few minutes ago?"

"Oh, because I knew he was going to have me do something for him. He never approaches me unless he wants something."

I chuckled. "Sounds like the story of my life," I said, and then I looked at Jillian's desk.

"Speaking of which," he said, and before he could finish his sentence, Jillian walked back into the office. She looked at me first and then she looked at Troy. "You know the rules, Troy. No fraternizing with coworkers, especially someone that just barely made it past their probationary period," she commented as she strolled over to her desk and took a seat in her chair.

Troy looked back at her, like she had just lost her damn mind. "Is that what you think I'm doing?" he asked her.

"It looks that way to me. But not only that, she has work to do," she replied as she shuffled papers around on her desk.

"Say no more," Troy said, and then he turned his attention toward me. "Thank you for the number to that eatery," he continued, and then he moseyed away.

I was a little puzzled by his choice of words. But then I realized that he had to say something to make it appear that he came in here for something other than flirting with me. I must admit that he's one clever guy.

"Done with the deposition yet?" Jillian wanted to know.

"I will be in a few minutes," I told her while staring down at my computer monitor.

"Well, I suggest you get to it." She wouldn't let up. This lady was truly riding my ass. There was no question in my mind that she didn't like me. From the first day I walked into this place, she had done nothing but give me a hard time. On several occasions, I wanted to bring her behavior toward me to Noah and Aaron's attention, but then I decided against it, for fear that it would trigger some backlash for me. And besides, I could handle her if I wanted to. Being in college taught me how to pick and choose my battles. This battle right here between Jillian and me was of no significance at this stage of the game. But if I woke up one morning and found out that I was losing sleep behind that tramp, then I'd have to reevaluate things. Until then, I would handle her with a long-handled spoon.

It became radio silent after I finished logging the deposition into the system. Once finished, I started sending out overdue payment letters to Noah's clients. While I was doing that, Troy started calling me. I had my cellphone on silent to keep Jillian from hearing it, but that nosey-ass heifer noticed how often I was picking up and putting my cellphone back down and turned around and gave me the evil eye.

"Why do you keep checking your cellphone?" she asked.

"It's my mother."

"Then you need to go on break and communicate in the lounge area. Not here at your desk," she scolded me.

"Say no more," I said, and then I got up from my desk and exited the office.

I knew Jillian was eyeing me down as I walked away, but I couldn't care less about her thoughts. They meant nothing to me. She meant nothing to me, and that was the way I intended to keep it.

I decided to go to the ladies' room, and while en route, I strolled by Noah's office. I could tell that he was on a phone call because no one responded out loud. But whatever person he was talking to was certainly feeling his wrath. I wished that I could see the expression on his face, but the wooden door to his office was closed. "You arrogant son of a bitch! I am the head of our brotherhood, and my brother sits on the board next to me. If you have any grievances, I am the person you address them to, not my fucking treasurer, you fucking moron. And if you continue to challenge me on the issue, I will uninvite you to our annual party," Noah roared.

Boy, was he giving it to whomever he was talking to on the other end of that phone. Mr. Noah was a beast, and the people he employed at this firm knew it too. I decided sixty days ago that I was going to get all of the knowledge I could from the twins, and when I was done, I was out of here.

While I was heading to the ladies' room, I called Troy and told him that I would be indisposed for a few minutes. He knew that it meant I was going to the bathroom and said I should save it and give him a golden shower. I didn't respond and he knew why. This wasn't his first time asking me to do this. Troy was a freak. He'd try anything. I, on the other hand, had my limits, and this was one of them.

The ladies' room was empty and I was glad of that. I hate sharing. On my way back out, I bumped into another junior partner at the firm. His name was Martin Colvin, a Markie-Mark of Markie-Mark and the Funky Bunch look-alike. Martin was a young white guy, a kiss ass for the twins. I never asked, but he looked like he was in his early thirties. A few times, I caught him making wisecracks about "black people in the ghetto." I never found him funny, but he had a few weirdos that would laugh with him. "Hey, Yoshi, what's up?" he asked, smiling from ear to ear.

"Hey," I replied, and immediately zoomed into the white powdery substance around the outside of his nostrils. "You got something white around your nose," I added. I knew what it was, and he knew I knew it.

"Really?!" he said, and tried to wipe his nose with the back of his hand.

"It's still there," I continued nervously.

At that moment, he raced back in the men's room. "Fucking lame!" I chuckled at the clown. After he took the second step, I saw that he dropped a small Ziplock bag of white substance. I started to call his name, but something tugged at my curiosity, so I picked it up, looked around to see if anyone saw me, and then I balled it up in my hand and carried on.

As I continued on to my office, I bumped into Noah's twin brother, Aaron. He was escorting one of his clients to the elevator. He and his client said "Good morning" to me and moved along. Before I turned the corner, Aaron called my name. It sounded like his voice was coming from behind me, so I turned around and, what do you know, he was standing in the middle of the hallway. "Hey, what's up?" I asked him.

"Would you come into my office for a moment," he insisted.

"Sure," I told him, and made a U-turn.

He waited for me to approach him, and when I got within arm's reach of him, he and I walked, side by side, into his office.

"Have a seat," he said as he pointed to one of the chairs placed in front of his desk. "How's your day been, thus far?" he added.

"It's going great," I told him. "What about you?"

"As expected," he continued, and took a seat in his chair on the opposite side of the desk. "I brought you in here to ask a favor."

"What is it?"

"I'm having a dinner meeting tonight at my home and I would like for you to attend."

"What kind of meeting is it?" I wanted to know.

"It's a meeting with a potential new client."

"What do I need to do?"

"Just be present. You know, sit back and look pretty. He adores beautiful women such as yourself."

"And what time is this meeting?"

"Eight o'clock tonight."

"Is there anything in particular you want me to wear?"

"Glad you asked. Put on one of those formfitting dresses I see models wearing. You know, the ones that make you look like you're on the runway. a little."

"I'm sorry, sir, but I don't own a dress like that."

"Oh, no worries, tell my assistant to give you one of the company cards on your way out."

"Oh wow, okay," I said, surprised. Now that's some boss shit there.

Mr. Aaron gave me a few more instructions and then he excused me from his office. I grabbed the American Express card from his assistant immediately after I exited the room. I flipped the credit card over to the back and then I flipped it back over to get a good look at it. Seconds later, I realized that I was holding the most prestigious credit card ever made. I could literally buy an apartment with this credit card because there was no credit limit. I was hanging with the big boys now and it felt good. There's only one way for me to travel and that was up.

After the meeting I had with Aaron, I wasted no time to tell Troy about it. When I entered his office, he was on the phone. I waited by the entryway of his door and waited for him to wrap the call up. I only had to wait a few seconds and then he gave me his undivided attention. "You won't believe what just happened," I started off my conversation.

"I'm all ears."

"Aaron just invited me to a dinner meeting at his home later tonight."

"What kind of meeting?"

"A meeting for a potential client."

"And he just invited you to be there?"

"Yep, and he just gave me one of the company's credit cards to go buy a dress," I explained, and then I flashed the credit card for Troy to see.

Troy's whole mood changed. "Are you kidding me right now?"

"No, I'm serious."

"Do you know what happens at those meetings?"

"No, but I'm sure you'll tell me."

"Sex. Sex happens at those meetings."

"Well, you know that's not what I'm about. And I don't think Aaron would invite me to that kind of a meeting."

"What makes you think you're so special? Do you know how many interns and secretaries this firm has gone through? Noah and Aaron use them to bait in new clients."

"Is that an insult or what?"

"I'm trying to get you to open your eyes."

"They're friends of my parents."

"Forget all of that, you're not going to that meeting, and that's all I'm going to say."

"I've already accepted the invitation, so I can't go back on my word. And besides, he's my boss, I can't say no to him."

"Well, you better make up a lie. And I'm done with this conversation."

"Troy, don't talk to me like that. The conversation is done when I say it is done."

Before Troy could make a rebuttal, Aaron's twin brother, Noah, walked up. He peered into the doorway. "There's been a change of plans."

"What's up?"

"Aaron has a new potential client meeting tonight and I want you to tag along."

"So the other meeting you and I had tonight is off?"

"Yes."

"Yoshi just mentioned that she was invited to the meeting as well."

"Yes, she is, and I know with her, you guys are going to bring it home," Noah continued, and slapped the door with enthusiasm. "Do us proud, you two."

I smiled. "Count on me," I replied.

Troy gave me the look of death. I could see his blood boiling on the inside from where I was standing. "Well, I guess that's my cue. I gotta get back to work," I said, and then I tapped the door and left. I knew I would hear his mouth later, but by then, he would've calmed down. Or at least I hoped so.

2
Troy

After Yoshi and I left the office, I made it clear in the parking garage that I didn't want her to follow me to my apartment. I wanted to be left alone. I needed time to mull over the fact that Aaron invited her to the dinner meeting to be held at his place in a couple of hours. I knew what went on at those meetings, but naïve Yoshi didn't. Her silly ass would find out though.

"So you're just going to leave and not say another word?" she asked me as she stood before me. We were both standing by the passenger side door of my black Porsche.

"There's nothing else to say. I told you to tell Aaron that you wouldn't be able to make it to the meeting tonight, but you're refusing to do that."

"Troy, he's my boss. I can't tell him no, especially after I agreed to go."

"Make up a lie. Tell him you suddenly came down with a tummy ache. Or tell him you got a bad migraine."

"Come on now, Aaron is a smart man. He's going to see right through that. And besides, he said he needs me there, so I can't let him down. I'm sorry, I won't do it."

"Well, suit yourself," I told her, and then I climbed into my car. She reached for my car door with intentions to prevent me from closing it, but her strength was no match for mine. And immediately after I closed my door, I started the ignition and drove away. I figured why stay there and continue beating a dead horse. I've got bigger fish to fry.

The Porsche I was driving was a gift from the firm. Aaron and Noah also had a car phone installed as a bonus after the huge settlement I scored for one of my clients and the firm. I was even given a cash bonus, but I had to give it all away to a couple of loan sharks I owed. It felt good to pay them. But I later fell right back in debt in less than two hours. Right now, I'm $250,000 in debt, and if I want to sit at another poker table, I will have to bring at least half of that to pay into what I already owed. Yoshi had no idea about my gambling lifestyle, and I didn't feel the need to tell her either. We'd only been dating for a month and a half, I think, so I still have time. Other than that, my life was an open book. Well, maybe 75 percent. You gotta keep some things close to the chest.

While en route to my posh apartment in lower Manhattan, I got a call from Jake, one of my poker card players. "Hey, buddy, still coming to Frankie's place tonight?" Jake wanted to know.

"I can't. There's been a change of plans. One of the senior partners at the firm ordered me to attend a dinner meeting with him," I explained.

"What time is the meeting?"

"Eight o'clock . . . eight thirty."

"It's five thirty now. You still have time to play a few hands. I can meet you there in forty-five minutes. We play a couple of rounds and you can be out of there by seven thirty."

"I owe Frankie two hundred fifty K. I'm gonna need half of that to walk through the door."

"I can spot you that. Meet me there in about thirty minutes."

I paused for a moment. Jake caught my hesitancy.

"Come on, buddy, you're wasting time. You can be in and out before you know it." Jake pressed the issue.

"Okay. Tell you what, I'll get in the game for about an hour, and then I'm going to have to retire."

"Sounds great. See you there," Jake replied, and then we ended our call.

Immediately after I got off the phone with Jake, I turned my car around and headed in the direction of Frankie's place. I had to get through forty-five minutes of traffic, but I made it there.

Jake was already sitting at the table when I entered the game room. He winked at me and told me to go to the check-in part of the room to get the chips he had already reserved for me.

Before I sat down, I watched the action unfolding with Jake and the other five players. Everyone received two face-down cards—the hole cards. The five community cards were then dealt faceup in three rounds, with opportunities for betting in between. The first card-up batch, called the flop, would consist of three cards. After that, I watched as the dealer added a single card ("the turn") followed by one more ("the river"). At this stage, players would vie for the pot by assembling the best five-card hands using their hole cards and the shared array.

Even before the flop, though, three of the five players chose to fold. Jake, who'd been dealt the queen of diamonds and jack of hearts, pressed forward with the hand. He alone was going head-to-head with Vinny Carmichael, a Sicilian from Brooklyn.

I noticed the flop contained the 8 of spades, 9 of diamonds, and jack of diamonds—a promising trio for Jake, who now had a pair (jacks) and was just a 10 away from a queen-high straight (8-9-10-jack-queen). There were two shared cards left to be dealt. The turn produced the relatively useless 4 of spades, after which Vinny slid a $5,000 bet.

As Jake grabbed $10,000 worth of chips in the pot, New York's most notorious gambler, Frankie Madison, walked in the room. Frankie owned this poker place. He also owned a couple of nightclubs and racehorses. He had such a formidable presence in the criminal underworld, his fortune had grown to an estimated $100 million. He was a high-level loan shark, liberally padding the pockets of police and judges to evade the law. He was known to carry around $200,000 in pocket money at all times. And tonight was no different. But he wasn't trying to spend his money, he was trying to spend what I had in my hands.

"Look what we have here," he announced as he stood before me.

I was holding money in my hands that Jake had spotted me to play at tonight's game, but that reality was slipping away when he reached for the roll of chips cradled in my arms.

"I came just in time," he commented.

Jake looked back over his shoulder. He knew Frankie had just entered the room, but my facial expression was what he wanted to see. After he saw it, he turned back around and continued on with his game.

"How much do you have there?" Frankie wanted to know. He was standing with his bodyguard.

"I'm holding this for my buddy Jake," I lied. I was not about to hand over the cash Jake just loaned me. He already paid half of my debt off to the house, and this money that I had in hand would help me win more money to pay off the house and give Jake his portion.

"Why isn't Jake holding his own money?" Frankie pressed. "Hey, Jake, why is another grown man holding your money?" Frankie turned his attention toward Jake.

"I can't answer that," Jake replied, refusing to take his eyes off the game in front of him.

See Frankie was a very feared man. But when he lends you his money, or gives you house credit, if you don't give it back in a timely manner, he becomes a mean guy.

"Well, Troy, since Jake can't answer my question, then I'm left to believe that money you're holding is yours. Now hand it over to me before it gets really ugly in here," he demanded.

"Frankie, I just paid the house one hundred thousand dollars. After I win a few hands tonight, I will pay you the rest of the money I owe you."

"What if you lose?" Frankie wanted to know.

"Trust me, I won't. I feel lucky tonight," I assured him.

"Do you know how many times I have heard you and every other man say that to me? You're sounding like a broken record right now. Doesn't he sound like a broken record?" He looked around the room and asked everyone in attendance. No one replied to his question, but a few of them chuckled and they turned their focus back on the game.

"Frankie, I'm a loyal customer. You know I'm good for it. I just paid the house one hundred grand."

"Troy, you've been owing me money for a while now. Your books haven't been cleared for months."

"But every time I come here, I'm clearing my debt," I pointed out.

"But I'm not making any money. I need players here that I can make money from. Not ones that play to pay off old debt."

"Come on, Frankie, let me do it just this last time. I could take what I have in my hands tonight and double or even triple it."

"And what if you lose? That means that you're going to be in more debt with me. And that will make me extremely angry, and I don't like getting angry. When I become angry, my mind won't let me get happy again until the very next day. And another thing, if I allow you to come into my establishment owing me thousands and thousands of dollars, and adding more and more debt to it, other players will come here and think that they can do it too. And if that happens, I would lose the respect I have, and everyone would come here and expect to get the same treatment. See, I run my business like a Fortune 500 organization. If you lose your money one night and come back the next night to get credit to win your money back, but you fall short again and lose the credit I lent you, then you have three chances to get out of debt. If you can't turn a profit with those three chances, then you can't play in my place until you clear your account."

"Listen, I just got two new clients. And the deals I have for them will net me one million dollars each and it could all be yours," I explained.

"I don't give a damn about your two new clients. Your chances to get the money you owe me just ran out."

"When did this rule start?" I asked. He had never mentioned this rule before.

"Listen to me, you gambling junkie. This is my place. I say *who*, *when*, or *what* when it comes to the rules and regulations. Now I'm gonna say it this last time, give me what you have in your hands, or I will be forced to whack you here, where you stand," Frankie threatened.

Everyone in this place knew that Frankie was a man of his word. If he said something would happen, then it would. I stood there and pondered for a moment, because I needed this money to generate more. But if I gave it to Frankie, I would be in more debt with Jake.

"I'm sorry, Frankie, but you're going to have to let me play at least two games." I rebelled and then I turned around and took one step to walk around the table to sit in the empty seat next to Jake. As I attempted to take another step, I was struck with a heavy blow to the back of my head. *Boom!* The next thing I knew, I was on the floor and the poker chips I had in my hands were scattered across the floor.

"Never disrespect a man you owe money to in his own house." I heard Frankie say. "Saul, pick up my money."

Jake helped me up from the floor. The guy Vinny, with whom he was playing, had won that round of poker, so Jake grabbed his chips on the table and began to escort me out of the room. "Come on, let's get you out of here," Jake insisted.

"My head is ringing and throbbing like crazy. My vision is blurry too," I told Jake.

"His bodyguard hit you with the butt of his gun," Jake replied, and supported my arm tighter with his arm. Every step I took, he took. We were arm in arm.

"No fucking wonder!" I commented as I tried to bear the pain that was pounding my head.

"Think you're able to drive home?" he asked me as soon as we exited the building.

"I think so."

"Are you sure? Because you don't look like it."

"Just get me to my car and I'll take it from there," I assured him.

"How much money did you owe Frankie?"

"One hundred and fifty thousand."

"You know that every time Frankie sees you, he's going to shake you down for whatever you got on you?"

"That's why I'm going to take my business elsewhere. I'm going to check out the spot uptown. I heard from a source that those guys up there literally throw away their money. Old men that just want to get out of the house from their nagging wives," I said while Jake continued to escort me to my car.

"Yeah, you've gotta be smart. Because what they do is let you win a few times and then they put the whammy on you and take you for every penny you have. Old men or not, their arms reach across every borough and they have eyes everywhere. And they have young guys on their payrolls that would snap your neck for pennies on the dollar."

"Oh, you're overexaggerating."

"Exaggerating or not, you need to stay away from these spots for a while. Pick up a few new clients and use their retainers to pay off your debts. Mine included."

"Come on, Jake, you're treating me like a bitch! You know I can hold my own. I got this poker shit down to a science. I only fucked up a few times."

"I can't chance that. You're my friend. I love you like a brother and I wouldn't be able to live with myself if I sit around and let you get caught up in this underworld of gambling. These guys would kill everyone you love, including me, because they know how close we are. So go home. Get some rest so you can get a clear mind," Jake instructed.

By this time, we had made it to my car. And as soon as he helped me into the driver's seat, he bid me farewell and told me to call him in a few days. I promised him that I would, and then he walked away.

I sat in my car for at least an hour before driving away. That's how long it took for the pain in my head to subside some. I mean, the pain didn't go away completely, but it felt a little less painful.

Instead of going home to get ready for the meeting, I went to the sports bar, a place I normally frequent to wind down. A crowd was there. I counted forty-nine people and the legal capacity number was sixty-five, so it was packed. I sat down on a bar stool at the opposite side of the bar so that I could see who was coming in and going out of the bar. There were three bartenders: two women and one guy. Brad was my favorite bartender because he wasn't stingy with the alcohol. He was a proud Irishman and made sure everyone knew it. To him, everyone was "mate, this" and "mate, that." He was a cool guy anyway you looked at him.

"So, whatcha having tonight, mate?" he asked.

"Give me a beer," I replied.

"Your usual?"

"Yep."

"Mate, one Modelo coming," he said as he pulled the bottle from a glass-encased cooler behind the counter. He took a bottle opener, flicked off the top, and placed the beer on a perfectly squared white napkin.

I picked up the beer and took my first sip. The beer was cold and refreshing, and after I swallowed the first sip, I took another swallow. My head was still throbbing from the excruciating pain from a blow caused by Frankie's bodyguard. I figured the drunker I got, the faster the pain would subside. So one drink turned into two, and two turned into three.

As Brad handed me the fourth drink, he noticed that I kept massaging the back of my head. He questioned me about it. "You all right?"

"Oh, it's nothing. I slipped on a piece of ice that was on my kitchen and bumped my head on the floor."

"Did you take anything for it?"

"Yeah, I took a couple of Tylenols. It'll go away sooner than later."

"Mate, you may need to get it checked out."

"I'll play it by ear. If it's still aching when I wake up in the morning, I'll go to the ER."

"Suit yourself," he said, and then he changed the subject. "Hey, you see that lady in the leopard shirt?"

I turned in the direction Brad was pointing and saw a gorgeous white woman with blond hair. She looked just like a Hugh Hefner Playboy Bunny. Her tits were huge. She winked her eye at me when our eyes connected.

"Yeah, what about her?" I asked.

"She just bought the beer you're drinking now."

"Oh really?"

"Yes, really. And, mate, she wants you to come over there and talk to her."

I held my beer in the air and winked my eye back at her. "She's pretty hot, huh?"

"Yes, she's fucking hot. Whatcha waiting for? Go and talk to her."

"I have a girlfriend," I said, thinking about what Yoshi would say if she walked in here and saw me speaking with that young, beautiful, blond-haired woman. It would crush her little heart.

"When did you get this girlfriend? Because just a month ago, you were picking chicks up and down this bar."

"I've been seeing her for about a month. We just got serious," I stated.

"Mate, did you and this new girlfriend get hitched?"

"No. Of course not, Brad."

"Well, then get your ass up and go talk to that beautiful woman over there. Thank her for the beer, for God's sake."

"All right, all right. Stop breaking my balls. I'm going over there now," I told him, and stood up from the bar stool. I grabbed my beer and headed over to where she was standing with someone I assumed was her friend. She smiled at me as I approached her.

"Thank you for the beer," I started off saying.

"You're welcome."

"So, what's your name?" I asked her.

"Paula. And this is my best friend, Amber."

"Nice to meet you both. And my name is Troy."

"Nice to meet you as well," Paula replied.

"I second that," Amber chimed in.

"So, what are you ladies doing here tonight?" I opened the floor for conversation.

"We both work at the gentlemen's club a couple of blocks away, so we're here letting our hair down and unwind before our shift begins," Paula explained.

"How long have you two been dancers?"

"I've been dancing for five years," Paula answered first.

"And I've been dancing for three years," Amber replied.

"What's the name of the club? I might just pop up on you guys one night."

"It's called the White Stallion. It's on Forty-Fourth Street," Paula answered.

"Oh yeah, I know where that is. I believe I've been there before. Wasn't it called something else?" I wondered aloud.

"Yes, it was called the Gentlemen's Playground," Paula told me.

"Yeah, yeah. I've been there. That's a high-class club," I added.

"Yes, it is. And we love it, right, Amber?"

"Absolutely," they both agreed, and *pinged* their champagne glasses together. "So, what do you do?" Paula continued.

"I'm an attorney."

"Attorney, huh?" Paula commented, and then winked her eye at her friend Amber. I knew what that look meant. They looked at me as an ATM. A man with the plan. A high-powered lawyer with endless amounts of money. But the real facts are, I'm in a lot of debt. Yes, I make great money as a lawyer, but I have guilty pleasures and they are creating a wedge between life and death. I can only hope to get my things in line before I end up taking a huge loss.

"Yes, I am a *lawyer*," I said, and then I took a sip of the beer I was holding in my hand.

"So, are you married, Mr. Lawyer?" Paula's questions continued.

"No, not yet."

"Have you ever been married?" Amber jumped in.

"Nope."

"Is getting married somewhere on your list of things to accomplish in your life?" Paula chimed back in.

"Someday."

"What about kids? Do you have any?" Paula added.

"Nope. Not yet. And if you want to know if I'll ever have some, then the answer is yes. I would love to have about two or three kids. Preferably, two girls and a boy."

"Are you dating anyone?" Paula pressed for more information.

"Well, yeah, kind of."

"What does that mean?" Amber slid in with another question. Whatever question Paula wasn't asking, Amber took up the slack.

"It means that I'm seeing someone, but it's not like we're getting married tomorrow," I explained to them both.

"Can you see me too?" Paula asked, and chuckled.

I smiled. "I see you now."

"I want to see you outside of this place," she stated.

"I work long hours."

"And so do I."

"You're not going to let me off the hook, huh?"

"Not if I can convince you otherwise," Paula said. "Okay, I'll tell you what. Give me your number and I will call you tomorrow. Maybe then we could compare schedules and see where we could go from there."

"Sounds like a great idea to me."

"Likewise," Paula said, and then she pulled a pen and a

store receipt from her purse. I gave her my car phone number and she wrote it down on the back of the receipt. Immediately after she wrote down my number, I thanked her again for the beer and then I headed back to the bar.

As soon as I sat back down, Brad made his way over to me. "I see you gave her your number."

"Yeah, she wouldn't let me leave unless I did."

"Oh, so you're Mr. Casanova, huh?" Brad teased.

"I'm just a regular ol' attorney trying to find my way in this world."

"I heard you're representing the CEO guy on a sexual harassment case."

"Yeah, he's a real scumbag. I'm trying to get him to settle. The young lady that's suing him has a lot of shit on him."

"I hear that there's more coming after him."

"I'm sure there is. Besides, he's rich. He can afford it."

"Mate, what I would do if I had all of that money," Brad commented as he looked toward the ceiling of the bar. He acted as if he could see the stars in the sky.

"Having a boatload of money only gets you in trouble," I told him.

"I don't mind getting in trouble. So, where do I sign up?" he replied.

We both laughed at his comment. In reality, it wasn't funny. There's a long list of people who would sell their souls for all of the money in the world. I, for one, have done just that. I make over $2 million a year at the firm, and I pay very little in income tax, and I can pretty much get anything, and I believe that it's all because I am a Mason. Once you're inducted or sworn in, there's no leaving the brotherhood. You swear to secrecy. You never question bylaws or the sanctity of the Order. To leave means to die as a Mason. While a lot of people think that our brotherhood is a cult, it's a union like no other.

Now over the past few years, some things have happened that I didn't agree with. But we are taught never to undermine or cast judgment against our brothers. It is forbidden. What goes on behind the walls of our meetings are never to be told. And if caught doing it, a Mason will be punished.

If I told my brothers of our chapter what happened to me tonight, Frankie would end up a dead man. So I will keep this to myself. At least for now.

After drinking another two beers and listening to stories about the people he knew in the bar, I lost interest in going to tonight's meeting and decided to retire to my home. I got up, told Brad I'd see him later, and then I exited.

3

Yoshi

After I watched Troy drive off, I got in the 1990 Honda Prelude that my parents purchased after I graduated from college. I thought about following him anyway, but then I decided against it. My mom always told me not to ever run after a man, because men come a dime a dozen. Not only that, but a woman only has her dignity, and she should always hold on to it. Now my mother may be a bitch at times, but she had a ton of wisdom, and that can't be bought. Who knows, maybe before I leave this earth, I'll become half the woman she is. In time, I guess I will see.

When I arrived at Bloomingdale's, I pulled up to the valet, got out of my car, and headed inside. I had an American Express in my hands with no limit and I intended to use it.

My mother had a personal shopper at Bloomingdale's. Amy was Asian, and she knew what was hot and in season. I stood in the women's department and waited for her. While I waited, I sifted through the cocktail dresses. I saw a few things that stuck out to me, but I wanted to look like a million bucks. I knew that Amy had the eye and knowledge to do it.

She greeted me as soon as she laid eyes on me. "Hi, beautiful," she said, and embraced me once we got within arm's reach of each other.

I smiled and hugged her tight. "Hi," I replied.

After we released each other, she quizzed me. "So, what are we looking for today?"

"I was invited by one of the firm's senior partners to a dinner meeting, so I want to look stunning."

"Is there a certain color you're looking for?"

"Black or maybe blue would be fine."

"Is it formal?"

"I think a cocktail dress would do just fine," I suggested.

"Well, then, I've got the perfect dress for you. Come follow me over here," Amy replied, and led me one hundred feet into the dress section of the store. She grabbed a one cross-strap black Nicole Miller formfitting thigh-split dress. My eyes lit up.

"Oooooh, yeah, that's it. I love it," I told her.

She looked at the dress tag. "It's your size too." She handed it to me.

I took the dress from her hands and held it out in front of me to get a better look. "It looks like it might be too tight."

"I don't think so. But try it on anyway," Amy insisted.

"Yes, that would be the smart thing to do," I agreed, and then she and I headed to the dressing room.

"Let me know if you need any help," Amy instructed after she unlocked the dressing-room door and let me in.

"Will do," I assured her.

It didn't take me long to disrobe and slip on the dress. I couldn't believe it when it fit me perfectly. And when I stepped out of the dressing room to show Amy, she agreed. "It looks stunning on you," she said.

I twirled around in front of the mirror to look at every angle of the dress. She was right—it was stunning. I knew I was going to be the eyes and ears of the dinner meeting. And regardless of what Troy said, I was going to prove to him that I was an asset at the firm, and I wouldn't have to open my legs to do it.

"Are you still dating that guy?"

"Yes, I am."

"I wonder what he's going to say when he sees you with a stunning dress."

"Who knows? He's a little pissed off with me right now."

"Care to elaborate?"

"He doesn't want me going to this business meeting."

"And why not?"

"He's afraid that the potential client will try to make a pass at me."

"Oh, he needs to get over it. You're a beautiful woman. What does he expect?"

"I ask myself the same question sometimes."

"How's your mother?"

"She's great. She's the one that hooked me up with this job at the firm. Well, actually, my stepdad. They've known the Weinstein brothers for over twenty years now."

"They're a big deal. They have a lot of fund-raisers. They give back to the community too. They also have a lot of pull in this town."

"They are great guys. And smart too. Sometimes when I'm sitting in the conference room with them, I become so amazed at how much these guys know about the law."

"Yeah, a lot of other attorneys in town know that if they go against these guys, they better have their stuff together," she shared. "So, when do you take the bar exam?" She changed the subject.

"In a few days."

"Are you nervous?"

"Of course, I am. A lot of people I talked to tell me that it is hard to pass the first time around."

"Oh, don't listen to them, you'll pass it. Just be optimistic and you will be fine. Tell me, are there any wedding bells in the near future?"

"No, not yet."

"Is this you talking? Or him?"

"We really haven't talked about it much. Now, if you want to know if he is the marrying type? Yes. But he has a lot going on, so I'm just going to let things play out the way it is supposed to."

"Have you guys talked about babies?"

"That question came up in the beginning. He wants kids, and so do I, but that's not a top priority right now."

"Just don't forget to invite me to either the wedding or baby shower."

I chuckled. "Trust me, you will be the first to know."

Amy and I conversed for another five minutes, and then I handed her the corporate card to pay for my dress. Once that was done, we headed downstairs to the shoe department so I could pick out an elegant pair of high heels that would complement my dress. Amy left me in the care of Maggie, and she hooked me up. I swear, it feels so good to go shopping on someone else's dime. It is the best feeling in the world. And to know that I was able to spend $3,000 on my attire, even better.

It didn't take me long to get back to my parents' apartment. I was surprised that there was a lot of traffic this time of the day. I was even more surprised that when I entered my parents' residence, my mother was ripping our housekeeper apart. "Dina, I thought I told you to get the dog's urine off the floor. Do you know, if I would've fallen, you would be out of a job?" my mother roared.

"I did clean it up. But Bruiser came right behind me and peed again."

"That is not a good excuse. I pay you to keep this place clean. So, if you gotta walk around this apartment in circles, then do so. I don't want this to ever happen again," my mother scolded her.

"Mom, what's going on? Why are you yelling at her like that?"

"Because she's not listening to me. Do you know that I almost slipped and fell down on the floor?"

"Well, thank God you didn't."

"That's not enough for me. I needed to make a point of it so that it doesn't happen again."

I let out a long sigh. "All right, Mommy. Have it your way," I said, and then I turned around and headed to my bedroom.

"Hey, what you have there?" she wanted to know, and followed me to my room.

"It's a dress and shoes for the dinner meeting tonight," I said aloud as I continued toward my bedroom.

When I entered my bedroom, I placed the garment cover on the bed and placed my shoes beside it.

"Oh, so you went to Bloomingdale's?" she questioned after entering my bedroom and sitting next to the packaging on my bed.

"Yep, Amy hooked me up. I have an important dinner meeting tonight."

My mother grabbed the garment bag with my dress and held it up, then unzipped it. As she unzipped it, she was able to see more and more of the dress. "Ahh, Yoshi, this is beautiful," she commented as she took the dress completely out of the garment bag.

"Mom, be careful. Don't get anything on it," I cautioned

her. She laid the dress down on my bed and took the shoebox out of the bag. "Gucci, huh?"

I smiled. "Nothing but the best."

"So, who's supposed to be at this dinner meeting?" Her questions continued after she sat on the edge of my bed.

"Aaron has a potential new client that's meeting him at his place to discuss business, and Troy and I were invited."

"That's awesome. Who is the potential client?"

"I'm not sure. But he has to be an important one, because Aaron is pulling out all of the stops to impress him. Troy doesn't like the idea that I was invited."

"And why not?"

"He wouldn't say," I lied. I tried to keep my mother out of my business as much as possible.

"Think he's jealous?"

"He may be. But I won't let that deter me from doing what I was asked to do."

"So, what time is the meeting?"

"Eight o'clock. But I'll get there around eight thirty, nine. I don't want to seem too anxious."

"I'm so proud of you. I mean, look at all you have been through while you were back at college. You held your head up, persevered, and now you're working at a prestigious law firm."

"I thought I'd never see this day."

"Well, it's here, and we have God to thank for it," she reminded me, then changed the subject. "How serious are you and Troy?"

"If you're talking about me and him getting married within the next year, that's not going to happen."

"Do you love him?"

"Mom, you just asked me this question, like a week ago," I protested.

"Your feelings could've changed from then to now."

"Yes, I love him. But I'm not head over heels for him. My focus is passing the bar exam and getting my law degree. Everything else takes a backseat."

"Smart."

I took both of my Gucci shoes from the shoebox and placed them on the bed so I could look at them and my dress at the same time. "Think I should wear stockings with these shoes?" I asked my mother.

"Of course not. Just shave those legs, moisturize them, and let those shoes do the rest . . . Are you ready to take the bar exam?"

"As ready as I'll ever be."

"Have you thought about what type of law you want to practice?"

"I'm leaning toward criminal law."

"But you make more money if you go corporate. That's what Noah and Aaron are doing."

"They do some criminal too," I informed her.

"Just look at you, you're so beautiful, smart, and charismatic. You can have the whole world if you like."

"But I don't want the whole world. I just want my life simple. Get my law degree, move further in my career, maybe get married one day and have kids."

"What you mean *maybe*? You better give me some grandchildren," my mother commented, and chuckled.

I smiled back at her. "Don't worry. One of these days, I'll give you a couple."

My mom pat me on my thigh. "Now that's what I'm talking about."

"I'm pondering the thought of moving to Miami."

My mother's expression changed quickly. "Are you out of your mind? What makes you want to ponder that?"

"Well, first of all, I have a couple of college friends down there saying that they love the atmosphere." I was exaggerating a bit. The only friend I had in Florida was Maria. "And I heard lawyers get paid a lot more money in Florida."

"That's it? Those are your reasons for contemplating moving?"

"I have more reasons," I assured her while trying to think of what to say next.

"I'm all ears," she said, giving me her undivided attention.

"The weather is beautiful there. Most of the people there are swimming in money—"

"You mean drug dealers," she said, cutting me off in mid-sentence.

"Mom, there are drug dealers here," I said, trying to make a point.

"Yeah, but they're more discreet here. What about the people on Wall Street? They have money to burn as well."

"Mom, you're acting like I'm moving tomorrow."

"No, I am not. I just want you to think about what's best for you. And Florida isn't the place. Okay, I agree, they do have nice weather, their beaches are beautiful, and there's a lot of money to be made down there, but it's a cesspool of drugs, sex, and murder."

"Okay, Mom, you made your point. Get out of here so I can get dressed."

My mother stood up from the bed. "I'm glad you're seeing things my way, because mothers know best."

"Yeah, yeah, yeah, daughters know what's best too," I added as she exited my bedroom.

The drive to Aaron's penthouse apartment on Fifth Avenue only took thirty minutes. After the valet driver handed me a ticket for my car, the doorman escorted me over to the concierge's desk to check me off on the visitors' list, and then I was escorted up to the apartment at the top floor. The elevator attendant informed me that there were only two penthouse apartments on the entire top floor, and Aaron and Noah owned them. It didn't surprise me, because together they both had a net worth close to a billion dollars. It seemed like everyone in the state of New York knew it.

The housekeeper opened Aaron's front door and let me in. I swear, the entire foyer and entryway of the apartment mesmerized me as I took in every square foot of this place.

"Mr. Weinstein and his guest are waiting for you in the cigar lounge," the Asian housekeeper informed me, and then she led.

I couldn't see the entire apartment from where I was standing, but I knew this place was enormous by the amount of wall space, huge oversized windows, and exquisite moldings. "Is that a view of Central Park?" I asked the housekeeper.

"Why, yes, it is," she answered, and continued to lead the way.

The walk to the cigar lounge seemed like it was taking forever, that's just how ginormous this place was. I couldn't believe that I walked by three fireplaces and we hadn't walked fifteen hundred square feet.

From the looks of it, this penthouse was fully decorated in a Victorian style. The rooms were grand with soaring ceilings. The pictures on the wall were historic, and I could tell that they were worth a lot of money.

After walking through half of the apartment, I finally walked into the cigar lounge, where Aaron and his potential client were awaiting my arrival. Both men looked at the doorway as I approached it. Aaron had just taken a drag of his cigar, so he immediately blew out the smoke and got to his feet. "Here she is, the lady of the hour," he greeted me, meeting me at the halfway point of the room. I smiled back and embraced him as soon as we stood before each other.

"Thanks for the invite."

"Don't mention it," he said, and then he grabbed my hand, lifted my arm, and twirled me around. "Doesn't she look stunning tonight?" Aaron added.

"Yes, she does. And she's even more beautiful than you described," his guest observed.

I smiled from ear to ear.

Without further hesitation, Aaron led me over to where his client was sitting. Immediately the guy stood up and extended his hand. I instantly sized him up. He was an older Caucasian man, probably six feet tall and of medium build. If I could guess his weight, he was probably around 190 pounds. And if I could guess his age, he was about fifty years old. From when I first laid eyes on him, I knew he was wearing a very expensive suit. I couldn't tell you the name of his shoes, but they looked expensive too. Aaron introduced him to me and said his name was Simon Howard.

"Nice to meet you, Simon," I said, and shook his hand.

"The pleasure is all mine, Yoshi." He exchanged pleasantries with me and then smiled.

"Want a drink?" Aaron asked me.

"Sure," I replied.

"Come, sit here," Simon said, and pointed to a seat between him and Aaron.

I sat down on what had to be the softest antique leather lounge chair on the market. The leather was definitely top-of-the-line, because only button-sized hardware was manufactured to hold it together.

"Are you a scotch girl or vodka?" Aaron asked me.

"I like them both," I lied. I mean, I could've told him that I wasn't fond of either and to make me a martini, but I didn't want to give off the vibes that I was difficult. I wanted to give off the impression that I was easygoing. And that I could adapt to anything. Aaron wanted me there to help him sway this gentleman into doing business with him, so I wanted everything to be perfect. And in the process, score points for myself.

"You are a very beautiful woman," Simon complimented me.

"Thank you," I replied, and then Aaron handed me the drink that he had made for me.

"There you go, scotch on the rocks."

I looked at the glass and forced myself to smile, because all eyes were on me. But what I wanted to do was pour it out and fix myself a Long Island iced tea. Now, I could drink at least three of those before getting drunk. Without giving it another thought, I psyched myself up and told myself that this drink was good and took my first gulp and swallowed. I swear, it felt like my throat was on fire, so I coughed. And then I tried to clear my throat. But that didn't work, so I coughed two more times.

"Are you all right?" Simon asked me.

"I will be in a few." Still trying to clear my throat.

"I thought you were a scotch girl?" Aaron chimed in.

"I thought I was too," I told him after finally getting ahold of myself.

"Want a glass of water?" Simon wanted to know.

"No, I'm fine. But thank you," I assured him, carrying on in a bashful way. I've been taught over the years that when you acted innocent and coy with older men, they gravitated to you more. It gave them a sense of pleasure knowing that they controlled you for the little bit of time that they had you. They wanted you to feel captivated and underneath their spell.

"So Aaron tells me that you are about to take the bar exam," Simon continued.

"Yes, and I'm studying every day. So wish me luck."

"You don't need luck. You seem like a smart young lady. I'm sure you will be fine," Simon added.

"Yes, she is a bright young lady. And after we groom her, she is going to be a force to reckon with."

The compliments coming from Aaron kept me smiling.

"Mind if I ask your age?" Simon asked me.

I hesitated for a second, wondering why he would want to know that. He noticed it too, and quickly recanted his question. "I'm sorry, did I offend you? If I did, you don't have to answer that," he said.

"Oh, you didn't offend me at all. And to answer your question, I'm twenty-three. Will be twenty-four next month," I told him.

"An attorney at twenty-four, that's remarkable," Simon added.

"Wait, let me take the exam first," I said, and chuckled.

"No, you'll be fine," Aaron interjected.

"Let's hope so," I replied. The energy of the optimism felt great, but I'm a realist, so putting the cart before the horse isn't a wise thing to do. I'm a play-it-by-ear kind of girl. "Have you spoken with Troy since you left the office?" I changed the subject. I hate being the center of attention.

"No, as a matter of fact, I haven't. But he'll be here soon," Aaron answered.

"Is that the other attorney you want to help secure the deal?" Simon asked Aaron.

"Yes, that's the one," Aaron assured.

"What deal are we talking about?" I boldly asked. I mean, Aaron did invite me here to help sway Simon into allowing us to represent him.

"To assist his company in negotiating the price and terms to design and build a massive shopping mall in Garden City, New York."

"That sounds like a very big deal," I commented.

"Oh yes, it is. Simon could stand to make two hundred million dollars," Aaron bragged.

Picturing that amount of zeros gave me a warm and fuzzy feeling. It also turned me on. I've never seen that amount of money before. Not even printed on a check. "Boy, do I envy your wife," I said.

Simon took a long pull on his cigar, then blew the smoke out of his mouth. "Aaron didn't tell you that I was a bachelor?" he finally replied.

I smiled bashfully at him. "No, he didn't."

"Maybe after we close the deal, we could celebrate and talk about the possibility of you becoming my wife," Simon suggested.

Taken aback by his flirtatious comment, I took a sip of the drink and turned my attention toward Aaron. I needed to see if he was okay with Simon's flirtatious behavior. Aaron smiled at me and gave me the head nod.

"Am I making you feel uncomfortable?" Simon pressed me.

"Of course not, and if I was, I would let you know," I said confidently.

Simon and Aaron both chuckled. "She's a firecracker, Aaron."

"Oh yeah, she's something else," Aaron informed him.

Simon took another pull on his cigar and then blew the smoke out of his mouth. "What kind of attorney are you shooting for?" Simon wanted to know.

"I would like to practice either corporate law or criminal," I told him.

"Aaron, I may have to steal her away from you. Hire her to work as my assistant, and after she passes the bar, she could work as my in-house counsel."

"Oh no, she's mine," Aaron protested.

I took another sip of my drink. It was so freaking strong, but I continued to drink it to show these guys that I could handle anything they pushed my way. After the fifth sip, I began to feel warm and nice. I began to smile more too. It seemed like everything around me was floating in the air.

"Whom would you rather work for? Aaron or myself?" Simon pressed.

I instantly felt pressured to choose between my boss Aaron and Simon. Both men sat there and waited for me to answer the question. And then they both burst into laughter. "You don't have to answer that, we're just teasing you," Aaron blurted out.

Hearing those words allowed me to sigh in relief. So to know that they were both pulling my leg took the pressure of choosing Simon over Aaron off me, and I found myself laughing with them. "I am going to kill you two," I commented.

For the next hour, Aaron, Simon, and I talked and laughed. They even decided to drink with me. The mood in that room was so relaxing. Aaron had his personal chef whip up cucumber and caviar wedges, lobster crostini, and lump crab meat salad. The food was delicious and I couldn't get enough of it.

"I'm going to steal your chef from you," I warned Aaron.

"The hors d'oeuvres are divine, aren't they?"

"Yes, they are," I replied, and stuffed another cucumber and caviar wedge into my mouth.

While I was stuffing my mouth, Aaron fixed each one of us another drink. "I can't believe that Troy still hasn't gotten here," I announced.

Aaron looked down at his watch. "I was just wondering the same thing," he chimed in, and then he handed me another glass halfway filled with whiskey on the rocks. I placed the glass down on the lamp table next to me.

"We didn't need him here. Your company was all Aaron and I needed," Simon insisted.

I blushed again. "You're so full of compliments," I told him.

"I only speak the truth," he assured me.

"So, does this mean that you're going to hire us to represent you on this deal?" I asked, giving him eye-to-eye contact.

"That all depends on you," Simon answered.

"Can you be more specific?" My questions continued and I took a sip of my drink.

"For starters, think I could get a neck and shoulder massage?" He got right to the point.

I didn't know how to answer him, so I looked over at Aaron. He hunched his shoulders, as if to say that the ball was in my court.

"Don't be afraid, I won't bite," Simon added.

"I'm not afraid," I said candidly, and then I took another sip from my drink. After I swallowed a mouthful of this liquid high, I stood up on my feet and walked over to where Simon was sitting. Immediately after I got within arm's reach of him, I watched him as he slipped off his dinner jacket and handed it to me. I laid it across the chair next to him. As I walked around the chair to get in position to give Simon the massage, Aaron stood up and excused himself.

"I'm going to go and leave you two alone," he announced.

"I appreciate the hospitality," Simon told him.

He smiled at us and said, "Yoshi, don't put him to sleep. We're going to need him fully awake to sign these contracts before he leaves."

Simon chuckled. "I bet you do," he commented.

When Aaron closed the door to his cigar lounge, I loosened Simon's shirt and dug into the muscles around his shoulders and neck, and one by one, I pressed down on them and tried to penetrate them as effectively as I could.

"Awww . . . yeah, that feels good," he said.

His comment made me dig in deeper. "Oh yeah," he continued, and tilted his head back, ultimately closing his eyes.

His moans and groans got a little more intense and I could tell that I was doing a great service. But then, I was getting restless. I knew the drinks that I had were taking effect on me, so I asked Simon if I could sit down for a moment. He happily obliged. "Sure, take a load off," he insisted. "If you want, I could return the favor and give you a massage as well," he added.

"That would be great," I told him.

"Now, I'm not nearly as good as you, but I'll give you my best," he noted.

"I'll take whatever you give me," I said, and then I let him have his way.

As he began to press his fingertips into my neck and shoulder, I was beginning to feel relaxed and intoxicated. "You're not half bad," I mentioned as I became light-headed.

"When you get regular massages and back rubs from spas on a weekly basis, like I do, you learn how to do it properly."

"That sounds fun," I said, and swayed my head back and forth with each pressure point of Simon's fingers. Before I knew it, everything around me went dark.

"Ms. Lomax, are you awake?" I heard a faint voice say. I thought I was dreaming until I heard knocking and it seemed too real for me to be asleep, so I opened my eyes. The sunlight beaming through the sheer curtains nearly blinded me, so I shield my eyes with my hands while squinting my eyes.

"Ms. Lomax, are you awake?" the woman asked from the other side of the door.

"Yes, I'm awake," I finally answered her.

"May I come in?" she wanted to know.

"Yes, sure," I replied, and pulled myself in an upright position. After I refocused my eyes, I realized that I had fallen asleep in what had to be Aaron's house, and his housekeeper had been sent to this room to wake me up. The room was enormous, and seeing the Asian housekeeper standing at the door of the room made it seem like she was one hundred feet away.

"Mr. Weinstein wanted me to wake you up so that you wouldn't oversleep and miss work," she told me.

"What time is it?" I asked her.

"Eight o'clock."

"Is Mr. Weinstein still here?"

"No, he left a couple of minutes ago."

"Is the other gentleman here?"

"Mr. Howard?"

"Yes."

"Oh no, he left a few hours ago. You're the only guest here."

"Oh wow! Okay, could you get the valet to bring my car to the front of the building?"

"Why, sure," she said, and then she exited the room.

I looked down at myself and noticed that I was undressed. But the dress I wore here was draped over the chair placed in front of the beautiful vanity. So I slid off the king-sized canopy bed I was lying in, grabbed my cocktail dress, and slipped it over my head. My shoes were on the floor next to the bed. When I reached down to grab my shoes, I caught an instant headache. "Fuck! Not a hangover," I said, and sat down on the edge of the bed.

I instantly jogged my memory, trying to think back on how many drinks I had the night before. With the way my head was pounding, the number was foggy. So then I tried to remember how I ended up in this bedroom. Who brought me in here and did they have their way with me? The thought of Aaron taking advantage of me made me feel dirty. But then I figured that Aaron could not have done that, because he didn't seem like that type of guy, so it had to be Simon. I mean, Aaron did excuse himself from his cigar lounge, leaving Simon and me there to entertain each other, so what if it was him? Did Simon have his way with me? Did he have sex with me while I was out of it? If he did, that's considered rape. So, did he rape me?

I knew the only way I could answer that question was for me to do a self-test. I eased to the edge of the bed, spread my thighs, and inserted my middle finger inside of my vagina. The moment my finger felt an excess amount of fluids inside of me, I knew it was a man's ejaculation, because it began to pour out of me. Confused, I sat there wondering: had I sent the wrong message to either of the guys last night? Did I allow this to happen to me? And if so, why? Shame and disappointment in my behavior took over me. What was Mr. Weinstein going to think about me? Was he going to think of me as a slut? A whore? And what if I screwed up his deal with Simon? Or what if word got back to Troy about what happened? He was going to leave me for sure. Doing this could also lead to me getting fired. Oh my God, what had I done now? I did know that, whatever happened, I had to figure out how I was going to handle things from here. And it started from now.

After grabbing my car from the valet, I headed in the direction of my parents' apartment. I knew that time was of the essence, and if I wanted to get to work on time, I was going to have to go straight home, take a shower, change clothes, get back on the road without incident. Getting home and taking a shower happened easily. But while I was getting dressed, my mother decided that she wanted to give me the third degree about my time at Aaron's house the night before.

"So, how did things go last night?" she started off as she stood at the entryway of my bedroom door.

"Everything went well," I replied while sitting on the edge of my bed, slipping on my knee-high stockings.

"What do you mean? Give me some details. Was Mr. Weinstein happy with your performance?" my mother pressed.

"Yes, he was," I lied.

"So, who was the guy? The potential client?"

"His name was Simon. He has a design and commercial building company. Aaron wants to represent him on a commercial deal to design and build a huge shopping mall," I told her, and then I stood up and slipped on a pair of blue slacks I had lying next to me on the bed.

"Will you be getting a percentage of that deal, once the deal goes through?"

"I'm not sure. Remember, I'm not an attorney."

"But you're working for the firm. And besides, Aaron did ask you to attend that meeting. And remember, he gave you the company credit card to buy that beautiful dress and shoes you wore last night."

"Well, in that case, you may be right."

"What did Troy have to say about the meeting last night?"

"He didn't show up."

"Whatcha mean he didn't show up? Wasn't he required to be there too?"

"Yes, but I think something happened, and Mr. Weinstein told him that he didn't have to come," I lied. My mom questioning me was starting to irritate me.

"Who else was there at the dinner?"

"Just myself, Aaron, and the client."

"Really? So it was just you?"

I grabbed my suit jacket and slipped it on. "Yep."

"I'm so proud of you."

"Thank you, Mom. I appreciate you saying that," I assured her, even though I knew that if she really knew what happened last night, she'd be angry and disappointed by my actions. My mother was a woman of class. I knew that she would've never put herself in a situation like I was in at

Aaron's home. I also knew that she wouldn't have ever drunk as much as I did either. Believe me, if I gave her the slightest inclination about what went on, she would scold me versus taking me in her arms and telling me that everything would be all right. So instead of allowing her to bombard me with questions about what happened last night, I grabbed my purse and car keys and kissed her good-bye.

"Drive carefully!" she yelled before I closed the front door behind me.

"I will," I yelled back.

4
Troy

Aaron had been calling my home phone and mobile phone since last night. The fact that I didn't answer it, I knew that he was going to rip me a new asshole when he saw me, so I braced myself the moment I exited the elevator on our floor. Natalie, the receptionist, had a message waiting for me the second I walked by her desk. "Morning, Mr. T. Mr. A. told me to send you to his office as soon as you step off the elevator," she said.

"Okay, thank you," I replied while dreading the conversation I knew I was about to have with Aaron. He was going to chew my ass off as soon as he laid eyes on me. Now would be the best time as any to come up with a good lie and hope that it was plausible enough that he would go easy on me.

Before I went to Aaron's office, I went into my own so that I could drop off my briefcase and check my messages. After finding out that no one called, I grabbed a random file from my desk, exited my office, and strolled over to Aaron's. En route, I strolled by Yoshi's office, and to my surprise, she wasn't sitting behind her desk. Aaron's paralegal, Jillian, was there. She was searching through the file cabinet next to her desk, with her back facing the door.

"Morning, Jillian, can you tell me where Yoshi is?"

Jillian turned around briefly. "She hasn't gotten in yet. Is there something I can help you with?" she replied.

"No, but thank you," I told her, and kept on toward Aaron's office.

Finally, after reaching the doorway of Aaron's office, I felt a sense of dread. I wasn't fond of getting lectured, and, unfortunately, that was Aaron's way of communicating with his employees. I knocked on his door and he instructed me to enter.

"What do you know? The dead have arisen," Aaron said loudly.

I chuckled and closed the door behind me.

"So, what happened to you last night?" Aaron's questions began.

I took a seat in the chair placed in front of his desk and said, "Had an emergency that I needed to deal with."

"Cut the shit and tell me how much money you lost at last night's poker game?" Aaron got straight to the point.

"Who told you that I was playing poker last night?"

"Just know that it doesn't matter what you do in this city, I'm going to find out about it."

"Well, if you want to know the truth, I didn't get to play. I happened to run into Frankie and he took every dime I had in my pocket."

"I heard that wasn't all he took. Word around town is that he gave you a couple of rights and lefts."

Feeling pretty lame by how I was just labeled, I tried to save face and poke my chest out a little. A man never confesses to getting his ass kicked by another man. That goes against everything you learned as a child growing up. "Trust me, it wasn't a one-way street," I lied once again.

"You hanging around in places like that doesn't look good for the brotherhood."

"Don't worry, I'm keeping my nose clean."

"I hope so, because we can't protect you if you're leaving yourself open. Do you remember when you had that problem with that guy that burglarized your mother's home and killed her? We made him pay for that, didn't we?"

"Yes, we did."

"The same thing goes for this guy that you just had the altercation with. If this sort of behavior gets back to the other brothers, they're gonna want that guy dealt with swiftly, and then you would be sanctioned to a rigorous probation regimen, following a mandatory hearing. It's not gonna end well with you. We are brothers of an elite group of men. It's very hard to get into our club. So we want you to treat it as such. Understood?"

"Yes, sir."

"Good. Now tell me how much money do you owe that fellow?"

I hesitated for a moment, thinking about whether I should lie or tell him the truth. I mean, he did say that he knew everything that went on around the city, so if he knew how much money I lost, why would he be asking me?

"I'm waiting," he added.

"One hundred grand," I finally said.

"Try one hundred fifty thousand," Aaron interjected.

I just sat there and looked at him, wondering what kind of game he wanted to play. "I want you to take care of that. And I don't want to hear anything else about it. Do I make myself clear?"

"Yes, sir."

"Now tell me what caused you to miss that important meeting last night?"

"The altercation with that guy caused it. But I'll make things right. Just tell me what I need to do."

"Fortunately for me, Yoshi came, played her position, and brought the deal home," Aaron stated.

"So the deal with Simon and the firm is a go?"

"Yes, it is. We sent the documents over to his firm this morning, he signed them, and had them sent back over."

"How did Yoshi influence him to go with our firm?"

"I can't say, because I retired early and left them in my cigar lounge."

"So she fucked him?"

"I wouldn't say it that harshly. I mean, like I said, I left them in the cigar lounge and they entertained themselves. And why are you so ticked off? If you were there, then you wouldn't have to ask me these questions. Yoshi was invited under the guise that she would be eye candy. You were summoned to be there to help bring this deal home. By representing him on this deal, you knew what his design company would do for us. But you weren't there to do that, so I did what was necessary, to convince Simon to come on as one of our clients. Now if you have a problem with that, you need to figure out a way to deal with it, because what's done is done. My brother and I are the senior partners of this firm, and what we say goes. Now if I ask you to come to another dinner meeting and you don't show up, I will fire your ass. Do you understand me?"

"Yes, I understand. It won't happen again."

"Good, now get out of my office. I've got a lot of shit to do."

Without saying another word, I left Aaron's office. My

blood started boiling after Aaron told me what had happened at last night's dinner meeting. How dare he insinuate that I was the reason why Yoshi fucked Simon, because I wasn't there. Was he out of his damn mind? If I knew that I wouldn't get fired, I would've told Aaron to go fuck himself. But since my options of other firms I could go work for were slim, I bit my tongue and went on about my way. I would deal with Yoshi and break off the relationship though. I didn't fuck around with whores and she demonstrated that she was one.

As fate would have it, while I was en route back to my office on the other side of the building, I heard the elevator door *ding*, so I stopped in midstep and looked in that direction. And what do you know? Yoshi was about to step off the elevator. My eyes turned bloodshot red. I was standing about ten feet away from the elevator; normally, at this distance, it would take a person ten seconds to walk to the elevator, but I leaped and rushed toward the elevator and got there within five seconds. This startled the receptionist behind her desk and Yoshi as she stepped off the elevator.

"Hey, you scared me," Yoshi stated. She gave me a cheap smile.

I had only known her for two months, but I knew the expression she'd make if she felt guilty about something. I looked down at my watch. "You're late," I told her.

"And you're going to make me later if you don't let me get into my office to clock in," she replied, and then she stepped by me and headed down the hallway toward the space she shared with Jillian. I started to walk away and go in the opposite direction, but my heart and pride wouldn't let me. So I sped in her direction and grabbed ahold of her arm and stopped her from walking.

"Ouch, you're hurting me!" she said loudly.

I looked back to see if anyone heard her and that's when I caught the receptionist looking our way. I instantly snatched Yoshi's arm and pulled her in the direction of her office. "We've got some shit to talk about," I told her while grinding my teeth together.

"You're hurting me," she said again, but quiet enough that only I could hear her.

My intentions weren't to escort her to her office, I planned to take her into the conference room only a few feet away, and that's what I did. Immediately after I pulled her into the room, I closed the door behind us.

"What is wrong with you?" she wondered aloud.

"Don't play fucking games with me, Yoshi. I know you fucked Simon last night." I didn't hesitate to say it.

"Who told you that?" she asked. I knew what she was doing by throwing a question at me. It was called *buying time*, so you could think of a lie.

"Yoshi, I know you fucked him, so tell me why you did it?" I pressed her.

"I didn't fuck him," she replied.

"Did you suck his dick?"

"No . . ."

"Yes, you did. Aaron told me."

"Troy, I didn't fuck that guy."

"Stop lying to me, Yoshi, and tell me the truth," I begged her. In a sense, I wanted her to tell me the truth, without telling me the truth. Actually, I wanted her to tell me that she didn't, and it would be the truth.

Her eyes became watery, and that's when she took a deep breath and exhaled. "Please tell me the truth," I instructed her as I stood before her. I could see that she was about to break down and tell me the truth.

"Troy, please let me out of here. You know Jillian is going to ride my ass all day for being late," she finally said.

"Fuck her. She can't fire you. I'll handle her if I need to. Now tell me what happened with you and Simon last night?" I asked her once again. I wasn't about to let her out of that conference room until she told me everything that transpired between her and Simon last night.

"Troy, nothing happened. Aaron made drinks for me and Simon, and then we all just sat around and talked. I asked about the deal they were working on and they told me. Outside of that, nothing happened," she explained.

But I wasn't satisfied with her response, so I put pressure on her. "Yoshi, I've been with this firm since I passed my bar exam ten years ago, so I know what goes on at those dinner meetings, which was why I didn't want you to go. Now tell me the fucking truth. Tell me what happened between you and Simon, because I know you fucked him."

"I didn't fuck him."

Without a moment's notice, the door to the conference room flew open and in came Aaron. He didn't look too happy seeing me with Yoshi backed against the wall, especially with her eyes watery.

"What is going on in here?" Aaron roared.

Yoshi wiped her glassy eyes with the back of her hands and exited the room, leaving me with the task of explaining to Aaron why she and I were in here. And why she looked like she was about to cry.

"I'm waiting for an answer." Aaron didn't let up.

"I asked her to do something, she didn't do it, so I started yelling at her and she started crying," I finally said.

"That's bullshit, and you know it. Tell me the real reason why she was so upset."

"That is the real reason."

"Troy, she doesn't work for you. She works for me. So tell me why she left this conference room with tears in her eyes."

"Because I asked her a question and she lied to me."

"What did she lie to you about?"

"A motion she was supposed to file for me." I was grasping for straws, because Aaron was right. Yoshi worked for him, so she shouldn't be doing anything for me. But coming up with the excuse that she was supposed to file a motion for me and didn't do it was a far reach, and I knew Aaron was going to call me on it.

Aaron stood there and looked like, *how dare you stand there and lie to me*, but instead of saying it, he laughed and said, "You're fucking her, aren't you?"

I stood there like a kid who just got caught watching a porno movie. I was exposed and Aaron saw it. He knew I was fucking Yoshi, and he knew that I'd been doing it for a while now. So I knew that I had to come clean.

"Yes," I finally said.

"Yes, what? I want to hear you say it out of your mouth," he badgered me.

"Yes, I'm having sex with Yoshi," I said, my words barely audible.

"Have I not taught you anything?"

"Yes, you have."

"Apparently not, because if you'd been listening, you would've heard the part where I say that the young women we have interning or come here to train for their bar exam are liabilities. They're only good for getting us new clients. That's it. Nothing else."

"Yes, I know that."

"No, you don't, because I can see it all over your face."

"See what?"

"You're pussy whipped," Aaron commented, and then he smiled mischievously.

"No, I'm not," I said defensively.

"Believe me, I know the look of a man who's pussy whipped,

and, my friend, you possess those characteristics. All I can say to you is, don't let her cloud your judgment about the business decisions that need to be made for the firm, because if I found you slipping, I will terminate you. Now is that understood?"

"Yes, I hear you perfectly clear. But can I ask you a question?"

"Shoot."

"Did Simon sleep with her?"

"What did she tell you?"

"She denied it."

"Well, then, there you go."

"But earlier in your office, you insinuated that Simon did sleep with her."

"I told you that I retired early and left them in the cigar lounge."

"What time did she leave your apartment?" Knowing what time Yoshi left his place would give me the answer I needed.

"Not sure. I told you that I retired early."

"So you can't tell me what time they left?"

"I'm telling you that I retired early and that's all I have to say. Now get to work before I suspend you and send you home for a week," Aaron threatened, and then he turned to leave the conference room. "Oh, and one more thing," he said after he stopped and turned his attention back toward me, "don't ever let me see you torment her again while you're inside this building. I don't care what you do in the privacy of your home, because that's your business. Just keep that drama away from my firm."

"It won't ever happen again," I assured him.

"You're fucking right it won't," Aaron told me, and then he exited the room.

After Aaron left me standing in the conference room alone,

I got a grip on myself and walked out of it, about twenty seconds later. I started to walk by the receptionist desk to let the bitch sitting behind it know that I knew she snitched on me to Aaron, but I decided against it. My focus was on getting the truth out of Yoshi, so I'd deal with that tramp in the lobby later.

5

Yoshi

I swear, I couldn't get away from that conference room quick enough. Troy just traumatized the hell out of me. I had never seen this side of him. Was he having an out-of-body experience? I thanked God for Aaron. If he hadn't come when he did, Troy could've hurt me pretty bad.

I turned the first hallway corner, and what do you know? I ran into Martin. He looked at me like he had seen a ghost. "You're just the person I need to see," he said.

I stood there before him, knowing exactly what he wanted to talk to me about. Surprisingly, this encounter with him displayed a white powder-free set of nostrils. He acted a little nervous though. I guess he was a little uncertain how to approach me about our last engagement.

"How can I help you?" I asked. I couldn't give him eye contact, because I was still visibly upset by Troy's antics.

"When you saw me yesterday, did I drop a small clear bag of Goody's powder on the floor?"

I pretended that I didn't know what the hell he was talking about. And up until now, I forgot I still had possession of it. I'd balled it up in my hand until I got back to my office, and from there, I had put it inside of my purse. When I got home to get dressed for the meeting last night, I took it out of my purse and stuffed it inside of my pillowcase. Talking about his Goody's powder. Goody's powder, my ass. That was cocaine, my white brother.

"I'm sorry, but no, I didn't see a thing. After I told you that you had the white stuff around your nose, I walked away and went back to my office. Maybe you should ask around. Who knows? One of the senior partners may have it," I replied. But in all honesty, I knew that clown was not going to ask anyone else about that bag of coke. He'd be a fool to do so.

"Are you sure?" he pressed.

I thought he might have some doubts I saw his little bag of cocaine and wanted me to fess up. But not this time. I would take that lie to hell if I had to go. So, there was nothing else to discuss.

"Yes, I'm sure," I tried to reassure him. But that didn't stop him from looking at me sideways.

"All right. Thank you for your time," he added, and then he turned around and walked away.

When I walked into the office Jillian and I shared, she lit me up about being late. I tried to tell her that I was on the floor, but talking to Troy in the conference room, but she wasn't trying to hear it. In fact, she got up from her chair and told me that she was going to confirm my story, and if she found out that I was lying, she was going to write me up.

Thankfully, Aaron stopped by our office as she attempted to go and look for Troy. Aaron somewhat blocked her exit as he stood in the doorway. He looked past Jillian and looked directly at me. "Are you okay?" he asked me.

I gave him a half smile. "Yes, I'm fine," I lied. I was actually feeling very shitty. I knew Troy knew that I slept with Simon, and I knew that Aaron knew I slept with Simon. The only thing that's fucked up about it was that I don't remember any of the details. I can't say whether that's a good thing or not. I did know that if Simon did have his way with me, then it meant that he raped me. But I can't say the word *rape* to Aaron. He'd fire and get rid of me in a heartbeat rather than lose a client like Simon. Simon was going to make Aaron and Noah a lot of fucking money, and I was sure that they wouldn't let anything or anyone interfere with that. It wouldn't surprise me if Aaron would stand up and rally against me if I ever brought up rape charges against Simon. The money these men had would buy their freedom, and I would be blackballed and would never get to practice law in the state of New York. And that was a fact.

"She told me that Troy held her up in the conference room, which was why she was late clocking in," Jillian stated.

"Yes, that's true. We were all in the conference room," Aaron confirmed.

Jillian looked back at me. "So I guess your tardiness is excused," she said aloud.

"She wasn't tardy. So fix her time sheet. As a matter of fact, since you did a really good job last night at the meeting, you can have the rest of the day off."

Hearing that I could take off the rest of the day, I felt a smile on my face. "Really? I can go home?" I wanted him to be clear.

"Yes, get your things and go home. Get rested up and we'll see you tomorrow."

I grabbed my things from the right drawer of my desk and then I stood up. "I truly appreciate this, Mr. Weinstein." I thanked him.

And when I looked at Jillian, her facial expression was out of whack. I could tell that she was livid that I wasn't going to work alongside her today so she could boss me around like her own personal slave. I smiled at her and said, "See you tomorrow."

"See you tomorrow," she replied, gnashing her teeth together. This bitch was mad as hell. And for once, it felt good to be on the winning side.

I walked by Aaron as I exited, and he smiled at me and thanked me again for helping him bring Simon on board with the firm. I started to ask him if I was going to get a bonus for my role at the meeting, but I decided now wouldn't be a good time. Besides the fact that Jillian was standing there, I didn't want to put Aaron on the spot. I'd get my chance to bring it to his attention.

The moment I stepped out of my office I headed straight for the elevator. I purposely avoided walking by Troy's office to prevent him from seeing me. I had had enough of his shit for one day, so getting out of here was what I needed to calm my nerves.

As I approached the elevator, Natalie got my attention. "Are you all right?" she sounded concerned.

I pressed the button for the elevator and then I answered her. "Yes, I am. Thanks for asking."

"Are you sure? Because it looked like Troy grabbed you really hard earlier. I'm the one that called Aaron and told him what was going on. I hope I wasn't out of line."

"No, you were fine. Thank you."

The door to the elevator opened, and as I went to step inside, I saw movement to my right through my peripheral vision, and what do you know? It was Troy coming my way.

"Troy, don't start again," I told him after he approached me in front of the elevator.

He blocked me from getting onto it, and he stood before me, grilling me again.

"Where are you going?" he asked.

"Home. Aaron said I could take off the rest of the day."

"You're not getting off that easy," he said in a whisperlike fashion. His teeth were literally grinding against each other.

"What are you talking about?" I asked for clarity, even though I knew what he was saying. It was killing him inside wondering if Simon and I had sex with each other. Anger and rage were visible on his face.

"Aaron told me what happened, so just tell me the truth," he pressured as he leaned in toward me. He didn't want Natalie to overhear what he was saying.

"Troy, I didn't have sex with Simon," I finally got up the gumption to say, and then I waited for his reply.

He balled up his hand, forcing a fist, and punched the office wall. It startled me. "Stop fucking lying to me. Aaron told me the truth, so why are you standing there holding on to that lie?"

When he punched the wall, Natalie nearly jumped out of her seat. Troy was definitely in a rage, and Natalie saw it. I thought that she would have called Aaron or Noah to come and defuse the situation between Troy and me, but she didn't move a muscle. I guess she thought that she would suffer a great consequence if she ratted on Troy again, which was why she hadn't made the call. When she didn't save the day, I thought one of the other partners would come out of their offices to see what was going on, but no one showed up. It felt bizarre to me.

"I'm not lying to you. I didn't sleep with him." I didn't let up, because I knew that Aaron didn't tell him that. Troy was trying to trick me into telling him something that I didn't know to be true, but I wasn't falling for it. He had to come harder than that.

"I'm going to give you one more chance to tell me the truth, and if you don't, then I'm done with this relationship," he threatened me.

Before I opened my mouth to speak, the elevator returned and now people started walking out of it, so I stepped by them and onto it. Troy followed me onto the elevator, but he remained mum until we arrived in the parking garage. When I tried to get into my car, he blocked me from opening the door with his body.

"Troy, please move so I can get out of here," I asked politely.

"So you're going to continue to deny that you let that old motherfucker fuck you?" he commented, and then he said, "You sucked his dick too, didn't you?"

"I told you that I didn't have sex with that guy. You're getting all worked up for nothing."

"Then why is Aaron letting you go home? So that you could get your strength back after all of that fucking you did last night?" he roared. The volume of his voice soared. I looked around the parking garage to see if someone was witnessing Troy's behavior.

"You better lower your voice before someone hears you screaming at me."

"I don't give a fuck about someone seeing me. This isn't about them. It's about you and me."

"You're a well-respected attorney, don't let someone see you acting this way."

"Between you and me, Aaron thinks you're a whore. He told me that I shouldn't care about whom you give your pussy to, because you're nothing. You're a liability and he will only use you to get new clients or to keep the old ones."

"I'm not trying to hear any of that. Just move," I told him, and tried to pull him away from the driver's side of my car. But he wouldn't budge.

"Did you just hear what I said? You're a liability to this firm. He won't let you work here after you pass the bar exam. You're just a sex object to those guys. They're just gonna use you up until the next intern or beautiful girl comes," he continued. I knew what he was saying was about me being a sex object, but the damage had already been done. All I could do now was change the perception of me and not let anyone put me in that position to sleep with a client for monetary gain. I mean, look at Jillian; she was still working at the firm, and from what I heard, she'd been working for the firm for five years. Okay, let's be honest, she was not pretty and she was probably thirty years old. But the fact of the matter was, she's still there.

"Troy, you are truly draining me right now. Please move out of the way so I can get out of here," I begged him.

He stood his ground. "Not until you tell me the truth."

I thought for a second and then I said, "Why don't you tell me why you didn't come to the dinner meeting? You would've seen that I'm telling the truth."

"I had some other pressing matters that needed to be handled. But this isn't about me, it's about you. It's about you making me look bad. It's about you fucking a white man, and now he's looking at you like a whore."

"I didn't have sex with that man," I spat. I was getting so irritated by Troy's constant badgering.

"So you're calling Aaron a liar?"

"Yes, I'm calling Aaron a liar. Now get out of my way before I scream," I protested. I was not giving into this guy, especially after calling me a whore. I refused to give him the satisfaction of allowing him to see how bad he was making me feel on the inside.

Fortunately for me, a white couple drove into the garage and parked their car three cars away from where my car was.

When they exited their car, Troy recognized them. They were new clients of his.

"Hi, Troy, is that you?" the woman yelled.

"Yes, Margaret, that is him," the older man said. He acted as if her delivery was embarrassing him.

The woman ignored the man, who I assumed was her husband, and started walking toward Troy and me. I was so relieved when I realized that lady was going to interrupt the game Troy was playing with me. And at that moment, I smiled and greeted her when she approached us.

She smiled and said hello. The man stood by the car and waited for her. "I know Jim and I are early for our appointment, but we got a call from John this morning wanting to know if you found the witness that witnessed the car accident? He's very worried that if that guy doesn't show up that the judge is going to take the side of the driver and passenger of the other car."

Troy stood there, not knowing what to say. He stood straight up and greeted the woman with a handshake and assured her that everything would run smoothly at court. She asked him another question, and while she was distracting him, I grabbed ahold of the driver's-side door and pulled the door open. "Take care of your business and call me later," I said very quickly, and then I escaped into my car. I swear, this lady could not have come at a better time. She gave me my way out of this parking garage.

I could tell that he was livid by the fact that I was getting away from him. It was written all over his face and I couldn't have cared less.

I drove back to my parents' apartment after leaving work. My mother was watching television when she heard me walking into the apartment. "Honey, is that you?" she shouted from her bedroom.

"No, Mom, it's me," I announced after I closed the front door.

"What are you doing home? I thought you went to work." Her questions continued as I heard her voice coming toward me.

"Aaron gave me the day off. He said I earned it," I replied.

"You must've really done a great job at that dinner meeting last night," she said as she approached me in the living-room area of the apartment.

"I guess I did," I replied nonchalantly.

My mother beamed with pride and pulled me into her arms. "I am so proud of you," she said.

When she released me, we both heard a knock on the front door. She looked at it and then back at me. "I wonder who that can be?" she said.

I hunched my shoulders, because I had no idea who it could be. I traveled alone on the elevator to get to our floor. In my mind, it had to be one of our neighbors.

"Who is it?" my mother asked as she walked toward the front door. I headed down the hallway toward my bedroom so I could take a load off. I really just wanted to lie down.

I heard my mother speaking with a woman at the front door while I moved around on my bed for a comfortable spot. Immediately after I found the sweet spot, my mother entered my bedroom with a vase filled with roses. She smiled. "Look what I have," she said.

I sat up in my bed, dreading to read the card she was pulling from the center of the dozens of roses. "You can put them on the dresser," I suggested.

"You don't want to smell them? They are a delight," she replied.

"No, just set them down," I instructed her, because I didn't want to play in Troy's game. Sending me flowers wasn't going to fix the way he spoke to me before I left work. I mean, how dare he disrespect me in that manner and then try to send me flowers like everything is okay?

After my mother placed the roses on my dresser, she tried to hand me the card, but I refused to accept it.

"You don't want to read it?"

"Nope."

"Why not?"

"Because Troy and I got into a heated argument before I left work, so this is his way of trying to get me to forgive him."

My mom sat on the edge of my bed, holding the card in her hand. "What happened, sweetie?"

Damn, I just stuck my foot in my mouth. I didn't want to tell my mother what transpired between Troy and me. Telling her that he's accusing me of sleeping with Simon wasn't something she would want to hear. She would definitely look down on me. She's big on women keeping things classy and respectful. More important, knowing that Troy called me a whore and a liability would make her look at Troy differently. She probably wouldn't invite him back to the house.

"He and I aren't seeing eye to eye on taking things to the next level," I finally said. But that explanation was far from the truth.

"What do you mean, *take things to the next level*?" my mother wanted to know.

"He wants me to move into his apartment with him," I added. I swear, this lying thing is coming to me very easy, and my mother was falling for it.

"No way. You guys have to get married first."

"That's what I keep telling him."

"Do you love him?"

"Mom, you keep asking me this same question."

"That's because you refuse to answer it."

"Yes, I love him," I forced myself to say. I wasn't interested in talking about how I felt about Troy. I just wanted to be left alone so I could get some rest and mull over the possibilities of how Troy and I would move on from this situation.

"Could you see yourself marrying him?"

"I don't know," I rushed to answer.

"Well, let's see what he has to say in this card," my mother insisted, and proceeded to open the card.

I watched her as her eyes sifted through the words; hearing her voice followed. " 'Hi, Yoshi, I had a great time with you last night. Let's have lunch soon. Sincerely yours, Simon.' "

Shocked by the words and the sender, I sat up farther in the bed.

"Wait a minute, do I sense a secret admirer here?"

Anxiety instantly filled my entire body. "No," I replied, not knowing whether or not I gave my mother a good answer.

"It looks that way to me," she disagreed, and slung the card at me.

I picked the card up from my bed and read it to myself. At first glance, the card seemed like a romantic gesture, but when I reflected back on the night and physicality of Simon, I was somewhat turned off. Simon wasn't my type of guy. He was literally old enough to be my father.

"It's just a card, Mother."

"Don't forget that he sent you dozens of roses," she pointed out.

"Mom, you're looking too deep into this. That man is old enough to be my father."

"For God's sake, I don't think he's trying to date you. His card merely says that he wanted to thank you for last night and he wants to invite you to lunch. Take advantage of this opportunity. He's a very wealthy and well-connected man. You could learn a lot from him. Maybe even work directly with him after you pass your bar exam."

"Maybe."

"Cheer up, this is a good thing," my mother insisted, and then she patted my leg with her hand. Two seconds later, she stood up. "Are you going to call him and thank him?"

"Yes."

"Good, do it. He'll appreciate it," she added, and then she left my bedroom.

I watched the clock for an hour before I picked up the phone to call Simon. I was hoping that when his secretary answered and told me to hold on, she'd come back and tell me that he was busy. But that didn't happen. He picked up the line less than three seconds after she put me on hold.

"Hi, Yoshi," he started off.

"Hi, Simon," I replied.

"So I take it you received my gift to you."

"Yes, I did. Thank you very much. The roses are beautiful."

"Will you join me for lunch?"

"When, today?"

"Yes, today. I've already run it by Aaron, that's why he gave you the day off."

Taken aback by Simon's confession, I just sat there, not knowing how to respond to it. Simon noticed my hesitancy to respond too. "Yoshi, you there?"

"Yes, I'm here."

He chuckled. "Oh, I thought I'd lose you there."

"Oh no, I'm here. I was doing something and took my attention away from you for one second. That's all," I lied.

"So, what do you say?"

"You mean about lunch?"

"Yes, this would really make my day," he insisted. But his words had manipulation all over them.

"Where will we go?"

"Do you eat sushi?"

"Yes."

"There's an awesome sushi restaurant on the east side of Manhattan and I know you're going to love it."

"What time?"

"I can send a car to pick you up around noon."

"What about one? I've got something I need to do for my mother. But after that, I would be free."

"Perfect. I'll see you in a couple of hours."

"Yes, so I'll see you then," I said, and then I disconnected the call.

Like an old nosey neighbor, my mother peeked her head around the corner of my bedroom door. She was smiling from ear to ear. "So you're going to lunch, huh?"

"Did you eavesdrop on my entire conversation?"

"Yes, I did," she admitted as she strolled back into my bedroom. "But why did you tell him that you needed to do something for me before you left?"

"Because I wanted to rest up a bit."

She stood at the foot of my bed. "So, how do you think the lunch date is going to go?" she pressed me.

"Mom, you're acting like I'm going on a romantic date or something. The guy wants me to meet him at a sushi restaurant. So we're going to eat, talk, and then I'm going to come back home."

"Are you going to tell Troy about the lunch date?"

"Mom, it's not a date," I protested. The sound of the word *date* sounded weird to me.

"Well, whatever you want to call it, just make sure you ask him a lot of questions and soak up all of the information you can from him. And remember this," she said, and fell silent.

"What?"

"You possess all of the qualities of a woman that could have the world in the palm of her hands without compromising your integrity. And if you remember that, the sky's the limit."

My, where did the time go? It seemed like as soon as I agreed to go to lunch with him, the car he sent was parked downstairs, awaiting my arrival. When I exited the building, a white guy standing next to a late-model Mercedes-Benz looked at me; we locked eyes, so I knew he was there for me. After he opened the back door, I climbed into the car and we headed into the direction of the restaurant.

The drive only took thirty minutes. When I arrived, I saw Simon valeting his convertible red Porsche. As I emerged from the car, he stood at the glass door of the restaurant and waited for me to catch up to him. He smiled from the time he laid eyes on me, up until the time we stepped out of our shoes and the hostess helped us both down on the floor.

"You're so beautiful," he started to compliment me.

"Thank you," I replied. I honestly didn't know what else to say. There was a huge elephant in the room and I wanted to discuss it. "Can I ask you a question?"

"Absolutely."

I took a deep breath and then I exhaled. "Did we have sex last night?"

Simon straightened up his face. He gave me a look of seriousness. "You don't remember?"

"Remember what?"

"You started kissing me and I told you to stop, because it seemed like you had a lot to drink. But you kept pursuing me, so we made magic. And don't worry, I went easy on you," he said, and smiled.

I instantly caught a lump in my throat. This fucking old man just said that we had sex, but he went easy on me! Was he sick in his head? How the fuck could he say something like that? That was some sick shit to say. I didn't consent to that bullshit, and he knew it. I swear, I felt like cursing him the fuck out, but I knew that if I did, there was no way that I was going to come back from it. Who knows? Aaron or Noah could fire me. Worse shit could happen as well.

"Are you all right?" he wanted to know, especially after seeing that my mood had changed. He knew that I didn't remember him sleeping with me. So now he was covering his ass and trying to control the narrative so that I wouldn't blow the whistle on his ass and say that he raped me.

"Yes, I'm fine. I just wished that I could remember the details. But if you said that you took it easy on me, then I'll take your word," I told him. But I saw what kind of game he was trying to play with me. Old men with power were always trying to prey on young women like me. This type of shit happened all of the time in the workplace and in business relationships. I refused to play the victim. I was going to take my mother's advice and play this fool at his own game, but I was going to come out on top.

Simon and I ordered a buffet of raw sushi and sushi rolls. This was my first time dining on the floor of a restaurant. It was quite an experience. Simon's conversation wasn't that bad either. But from time to time, I couldn't get it out of my mind that this white man took advantage of me while I was vulnerable. Troy was right, this guy looked at me as a whore. He saw me as an easy target, a liability, and there was nothing I could do to change it. I guess the only thing I could do was pretend to like him and suck him dry for as much as I could.

"Are you dating anyone?"

"No," I lied. I couldn't tell him that Troy and I were seeing each other. That information would get back to Aaron quicker than I could blink an eye. Besides that, I didn't want this guy in my business. I figured, the less he knew about me, the better I'd be.

"No one?" he asked. He was giving me the impression that he knew I was seeing Troy, but I stuck to my guns.

"Nope. But why do you ask?"

"Because I would like to see you again."

"See me again, why?"

"Because you're beautiful. I like your company. And I know that in my line of work and the friends I have, you're like forbidden fruit."

"Are you married? Seeing anyone?" I threw the questions back at him.

"I'm recently divorced."

"Kids?"

"Two."

"How old?"

"Let's just say that they're both in college. My daughter is at Harvard. And my son is attending Yale."

"Names?"

"That's not important."

"Why not?"

"Because it wouldn't be appropriate," he stated.

And I was totally confused by it. I wanted to dig further, but then I decided against it.

"I wonder what they would say if they saw me with their father?" I commented.

"They wouldn't see you."

"But you said that you'd like to see me again."

"Yes, me. Not them," he corrected.

Once again, this old guy had shocked me by his comments. He was one clever guy.

"So, when you say you would like to see me again, what did you have in mind?"

"We would have an arrangement."

"What would that *arrangement* look like?" I pressed him. I needed more details.

"If things work out between us, I would see you a certain number of days on a weekly basis. I would put you in an apartment. Provide you with transportation."

"I already have a car."

"Well, in that case, I would provide you with a spending allowance on a weekly basis and we would have sex."

"So I would be at your beck and call?"

"I wouldn't quite put it in those words, but yes."

"Would I still be able to work at the firm?"

"Of course. But after you take your bar exam, I would prefer you work for me."

"Who would know about this arrangement?"

"Just you and me. Well, my assistant, Mario, would know. He would be your go-to person when you need to reach me."

"What if you fell in love with me and wanted to share it with the entire world?"

"That will never happen."

"How can you be so sure?"

"Because I am a man of prestige and influence. Being seen, arm in arm, with you would affect me in a negative fashion."

"But I don't understand."

"The kind of people I work with, and do business with, are very conservative people. They adhere to the old fabric of our nation. They frown upon mixed-raced couples. And I sort of believe in that institution, but some black women I find beautiful. You're like forbidden fruit, and it gives me a rush just being in your presence."

When Simon finished his statement about mixed-raced couples, I was utterly offended. I mean, how dare he talk about black people. But then, when I thought about it, his beliefs and those of other people in his circle, it's the same thing in my community. The only difference was, he was a very wealthy man, so he could afford to sneak around with women of my ethnicity. I wondered if I was the first black woman he wanted to sow his royal oats with?

"You really thought this out, huh?"

"When I first laid eyes on you last night, I knew that I had to have you in my life in some capacity. And then when I made love to you last night, that's when I knew for sure."

"Would the Weinstein brothers know about this?"

"No. Like I said before, it would be you, myself, and my assistant."

"This assistant you talk about, I take it that you trust him?"

"Absolutely. He's been working for me for over twelve years. I trust him with my life."

"That's truly brave to say."

"It's the truth. You don't have anyone that you can trust with your life?"

I thought for a second. "Maybe my parents. But that's it."

"Both of my parents are deceased."

"Sorry to hear that."

"Don't be. They weren't good parents. Well, at least my father wasn't." He spoke like he had a bad taste in his mouth when he spoke of his parents.

One part of me wanted to ask him why he felt the way he did, but then I figured why would I want to know. He meant nothing to me, so it would be wasted conversation.

"So, where did you go to school?" he changed the subject.

"For my undergrade, Old Dominion University. And Regent University for law."

"Where is that?"

"In Virginia."

"Did you like it there?"

"It was okay, until I lost one of my roommates to suicide."

"Sorry to hear that."

"It was a tragedy. She was a very nice girl."

"Why did she commit suicide?"

"She took a lot of prescription drugs at one time."

"Wow! That's unfortunate."

"Yeah, tell me about it. I was here in New York when it happened."

"It's rough when you can be at a number of places, all at the same time," he said, and then he asked me, "Have you ever wanted to commit suicide?"

I swear, that question had to have come out of left field. What an insensitive question that was! I had only known this guy for twenty-four hours, so why did he think it was okay to ask me that kind of question? And what possessed him to think that I would answer him, if, in fact, I had?

"Of course not," I finally answered. And I answered in a way to let him know that I was offended by the question.

"Wait, did I say something wrong?"

"Of course, you did. What would make you ask me that? Do I come across as a girl that would take her own life?"

"No, as a matter of fact, you don't. I was just merely being inquisitive. Nothing more. So allow me to apologize."

"I accept your apology," I said, and then I took a sip of the hot tea sitting before me.

"Are you excited by becoming a lawyer?" he changed the subject.

I'm glad he did, because another elephant was about to emerge.

"I am, but I'm petrified by the thought of failing the exam, which, of course, would force me to take it again."

"Don't worry. Aaron and Noah are some fine and smart attorneys. You just make sure that you learn as much as you can from them and you'll be fine."

Simon and I talked and ate sushi for over an hour and a half. When it was time to go our separate ways, he promised that he'd give me a call the following day so that we could talk and get to know each other more. I really didn't care one way or another. I had a lot of shit to take care of in my own drama-filled life: Troy being one of those things. It wouldn't surprise me if he'd been blowing my parents' phone up. I guess I would see when I returned home.

Before we parted ways, Simon kissed me on the cheek. It felt yucky. I immediately wiped his saliva off after climbing back into the car that I had arrived in. The driver saw it from his rearview mirror and laughed.

"I take it you didn't like the kiss?"

"It was too wet."

"You're a beautiful woman. You may have intimidated him."

"Thank you. But if I intimidate him, then why kiss me?"

"Why not?" the driver said, and then he put the car in gear and made his way into the street traffic.

I thought about his answer as he drove away from the restaurant and it made little sense to me. So I laid my head against the headrest and thought about all of the events that took place today. If only Troy knew that I had lunch with Simon today—boy, would he kill me!

When I finally arrived home, my mother told me that Troy called at least a dozen times. She even told me that he wondered where I was.

"What did you tell him?" I asked her while standing in the foyer of the apartment with my purse clutched in my hands.

"I told him that you were out running errands," my mother told me. "He seemed very angry. And I don't think he believed me," she added.

"I'll call him back in a few minutes," I replied, and moved past her so that I could go to the bathroom.

She followed me. "So, how was the lunch?" she wanted to know.

"It was nice. The food was great."

"What did you guys talk about?"

"He wants to see me again, Mom. He said that he wants to give me an allowance so that I can buy anything I want, and after I take the bar exam, he wants me to come and work for him." I told her all of this while continuing to walk in the direction of the bathroom.

"Okay, so I like the working-for-him part, but the other parts sound like he wants a trophy piece to walk around with. Is he married?"

"No. He says that he's divorced," I added as I entered the bathroom. By the time I placed my purse down on the sink and removed my pants to sit down on the toilet, my mother stood on the other side of the door with more questions.

"What about children?"

"He has two. They're both in college."

"That's not good. I mean, how would that look? You and his children are around the same age. Trust me, it would never work. His kids would give him a very hard time after they found out that you two were dating. And what about Troy? He would be crushed if he found out that you were seeing that older man."

"The older man's name is Simon. And Simon doesn't want anyone other than me, him, and his assistant to know about this relationship. I would be like his mistress, but without him being married."

I heard my mother let out a long sigh. "What are your thoughts about this?"

"Mom, I don't have any thoughts at this moment. I really don't want to talk about it."

"Well, if you want my opinion, I don't like that arrangement at all. You're worth more than he'll ever know."

"Yes, Mom, I know."

"Well, did you tell him that?"

"In so many words, I did," I lied. I couldn't let my mother

know that I entertained the idea of his proposal. She would be devastated.

"Well, I hope you do the right thing. Remember, you possess all of the qualities to write your own ticket without compromising your integrity."

"Yes, Mom, I know."

"Good," she said, and then I heard her walk away from the bathroom door.

6
Troy

I've called Yoshi over a dozen times, and each time I call her, her mother or the housekeeper tells me that she's not there. Well, guess what? I don't believe them, so I'm leaving the court building right now and heading over to her parents' apartment.

"Troy, what's going on?" a voice from behind asked me while I was unlocking my car door to climb inside.

I turned around and there, standing in front of me, were two white guys. They both looked familiar, dressed in all black. "I'm doing fine. How can I help you guys?" I asked them while trying to jog my memory about where I knew them.

Without saying a word, both guys started attacking me, throwing both fists at me. I tried using my briefcase to shield the blows, but my briefcase was no match for them. "What do you guys want?" I started shouting, and then I started yelling for help. I was in the parking garage next to the county court offices, and no one could hear me.

"You've been paid a lot of money and yet you did a shitty job in court today. You promised to get our boss bail and you failed," one guy growled as both men continued throwing one blow after the next.

"I know. I know. I'm going to put in an appeal tomorrow," I replied after losing my briefcase. It fell to the ground and all my paperwork and important documents started flying out of it. I even tried to run, but the grip they had on me was too strong.

"No, you're going to do it today," the same guy said.

"Yeah, you piece of shit! You're going to file the paperwork today," the other guy roared as he grabbed my neck and applied pressure to it. I started choking uncontrollably.

"Okay, I will. Just let me go and I'll go and do it now," I begged. The blows coming from their fists stung me hard every time they connected to my face and stomach, and that's when I collapsed on the ground.

"You're fucking right, you are," the same guy said. His words were menacing as he kicked and stomped me.

"Hey, what are you guys doing?" I heard a man's voice coming from fifty feet away.

I couldn't see the man, but I heard his feet running in my direction. And at that moment, the guys released me and started running away on foot.

My body was weak from all of the punches it endured. I curled up in a fetal position. I noticed my left eye was slowly closing up too.

When the guy finally approached me, I realized who it was. He knew me and I knew who he was. His name was Dwight and he was one of the older black deputies of the courts. He had his things in hand, like he was about to get in his car and go home. "Hey, you all right?" was the first thing he asked.

"They beat me up pretty bad, huh?" I commented.

"Yeah, it looks that way. Think you could stand up on your feet if I help you up?" he wanted to know.

"I'm sure I can," I said, cradling my stomach with both of my arms.

"Okay, I'm going to count to three and then I'm going to lift you up," he warned as he hunched down and locked both of his arms around my armpits.

"Got it."

"One, two, three," the deputy said, and then he lifted me up.

"Ogggggg!" I squealed. The pain was excruciating. But this was the only way that I was going to get off the ground. When I was finally standing up on both feet, the deputy opened my car door and placed me in the driver's seat. I instantly looked in the rearview to get a look at my face. Blood was everywhere and my eyes were swollen.

"You're not going to be able to drive out of here. I'm gonna have to call the paramedics," he insisted.

"It looks like I'm going to need to get some stitches."

"Yeah, it does look that way," he agreed. "Does that phone in your car work?"

"Yes, it does," I told him, and grabbed the base of it.

"Dial 911. And I'll talk to them. That way, you don't get the phone bloody," he instructed.

Immediately after I dialed 911, I handed him the receiver. He hunched down near the driver's-side door to make sure he didn't stretch the cord. "Hi, ma'am, my name is Deputy Dwight Fisher and I'm standing next to a gentleman that needs the care of the paramedics."

I couldn't hear what the woman was saying, but I was sure that she was asking him the appropriate questions to get as much information as she could so that she'd send out the right people to help me.

"We're standing in the east parking garage of the general

district court. And we're on level four," he said, and fell silent.

"He has been beaten up badly. And it looks like there's an open flesh wound above his left eye, so I know that it's gonna need stitches," he continued, and once again waited for the operator to speak.

"Yes, he's conscious," he noted. "She wants to know if you knew the guys that attacked you?"

At first thought, I was going to say yes, but then I knew that if I had, I could potentially put my life in further danger. The guys that attacked me worked for a client I represented. The client's name was Eric Young. And Eric Young was a pimp. A very violent one, I might add, and he's rich and feared on the streets of Harlem. So far, he has paid me a retainer of $50,000 and I promised to get him out of jail and keep him out of jail until we go to trial on four counts of endangering a minor, three counts of assault with a deadly weapon, and four counts of holding minors against their will. In essence, Eric Young kidnaps girls and runs a prostitution ring. Word has it, this guy makes at least $100,000 a night with his girls. So sitting in jail prevents him from running his empire. And by sending his guys to rough me up sends a clear message that he was not happy with my performance today.

I will admit this. The main reason I didn't do so well in court was because of Yoshi's actions with Simon. She's telling me that she didn't sleep with the guy, but I know better. And that's why I couldn't represent my client effectively today. I can't get my mind off Yoshi.

"No, I didn't know the guys," I finally answered.

"He said that he didn't know the attackers," the deputy told the 911 dispatcher.

The deputy finished the call by telling the operator my full name and what color car we were standing by. After he disconnected the call, he started asking a series of questions, like he was a fucking detective. This made me extremely uncom-fortable.

"Are you sure that you didn't know those guys? Because I believe I heard one of them saying that you're going to file an appeal today."

Shocked by his question, I quickly tried to gather my thoughts and come up with a plausible answer. I mean, I am a lawyer, so that shouldn't be hard to do. But, thankfully, my car phone rang and saved me from burying myself in a bucket of lies.

"Sounds like someone's calling you," the deputy pointed out.

I reached for the phone and held it a couple of inches from my face so that my blood wouldn't get on it. "Hello," I an-swered.

"Troy, this is Yoshi. My mother told me that you've been calling the house for me." After I heard her voice, the anger I felt in my heart for her evaporated into thin air.

"Yoshi, thank you for calling me back," I told her while I watched the deputy try to grab all of my important docu-ments from the ground and stuff them back in my briefcase. When he grabbed all of the papers he could find, he placed my briefcase on the hood of my car.

"What's wrong? You sound troubled."

"I was just attacked by two guys in the parking garage next to the general district court offices."

"What do you mean you were *attacked*? Are you hurt?" she wondered aloud.

"Yes, I was beat pretty bad, and the paramedics are on their way to take me to the hospital, so meet me there."

"What hospital?"

"New York Presbyterian Hospital on Praveen Hospital Lane Sixty-Eighth Street," I said, and within seconds, the paramedics' siren started roaring in the background.

"Is that the paramedic I hear?"

"Yes, that's them," I said while the sirens were blaring in my ear.

"You're going to have to hang up with her, because they're driving up now," the deputy instructed me.

"I've gotta go, baby. Meet me at the hospital."

"I'm on my way there now," she assured me, and then I disconnected our call.

As soon as the vehicle stopped, two paramedics jumped out with their bags and rushed over to where I was sitting. The deputy stepped to the side to give the paramedics room to work on me.

"Do you guys need me for anything else?" the deputy asked the paramedics.

"No, we've got it from here. Thank you for waiting around," the male paramedic replied.

"Take care of yourself," the deputy told me.

"Will do. And thanks for saving my life," I added. I didn't see the deputy get in his car and drive away, but I heard the muffler as it *put-putted* away.

"Can you see the light?" the female paramedic questioned me as she pointed a small flashlight in both of my eyes.

"I can see in my right eye, but my left eye is losing sight."

The male paramedic started cleaning the blood that continued to ooze from the flesh wound around my eye. It throbbed as he applied pressure with a handful of clean gauzes.

"Ouch," I whined.

"Where else are you hurting?" the woman wanted to know.

"I got punched and kicked really bad in my stomach and chest area."

"Can you walk to the ambulance?" she questioned.

"Yes."

"Come on and let's get you to the hospital," she said.

The male paramedic lifted me up on my feet and escorted me to the vehicle, while the woman grabbed my briefcase and car keys. "I'm going to lock your car door, okay?"

"Yes, that's fine. But will you grab the mobile phone from my car too?" I asked her while being escorted to the ambulance.

"Sure," she said, and retrieved it with my other things.

The male paramedic and I climbed in the back of the ambulance, while the female paramedic climbed in the driver's seat. I heard her radio the hospital, and when she got confirmation that she could take me there for treatment, she put the gear in drive and made her way out of the parking garage.

"Can you take me back to how this attack happened?" the paramedic asked as he took my blood pressure.

"Two guys approached me and tried to rob me, and when I put up a fight, they attacked me," I started off saying. This lie definitely seemed plausible, especially since I was wearing a Rolex watch and was driving a Porsche.

"Did they have a gun?"

"If they did, they didn't use it."

"Thank God. Because if they did have one and used it, you could've easily been getting transported in a coroner van instead of this ambulance."

"Yeah, thank God!"

7

Yoshi

"Has something happened to Troy?" my mother, rushing to my bedroom, asked.

"Yes, he's on his way to the hospital. He said that he was attacked by two men in the parking garage next to the courts," I explained as I grabbed my things and made my way by my mother, who was standing at the entryway of my bedroom.

"Oh my God! I hope he's all right." She followed me down the hallway that led to the front door.

"I hope so too. I'll call you after I get to the hospital," I told her.

"Please do," she replied, and watched me as I exited the apartment.

The drive to New York Presbyterian didn't take long. Unfortunately for me, they didn't have valet parking. I had to circle the block at least a dozen times to find a parking space. I became increasingly frustrated with the limited spaces of parking, especially if you had a certain amount of time to get into the hospital to see your loved one. The fortunate part was that Troy hadn't been shot, so his odds of surviving his wounds were very high.

When I entered the hospital, I raced over to the information desk and got the receptionist to help me find Troy. I was instructed to go to the emergency room and there I laid eyes on Troy. He was so happy to see me. But I wasn't happy to see how beat up he was. I rushed to his side and hugged him.

"Ouchhh!" he yelled when I bear-hugged him.

I released my grip on him. "I'm sorry."

"No, it's cool. I'm just in a lot of pain."

"I see," I said as I stepped back to get a better look at him. His face was pretty bruised up. There were at least seven cuts on his face and neck area. One of his eyes was completely shut. The other eye looked like a blood vessel had burst inside it. "Now tell me what happened?" I asked.

"Two guys came out of nowhere and started attacking me. I tried to defend myself, as much as I could, but I was no match for them."

"Why did they attack you?"

"They were a couple of mob guys that work for a guy I'm representing on a bunch of counts of running a child prostitution ring and holding underage girls against their will. You name it, he has been charged with it. Anyway, I promised him that I would get him a bail hearing and get him out of jail, and I only made the first one happen, so he got his goons to follow me into the parking garage, out of everyone's sight, and attack me."

"That's horrible. Is that legal? I mean, can they do that?"

"Of course, it's not legal. But look at what kind of people I am dealing with."

"You're going to press charges, right?"

"Do you know what will happen to me if I did?"

"Get a restraining order."

"A restraining order will not protect me, Yoshi. I've gotta get that guy out of jail."

"But he's a freaking pimp. Selling little girls to the highest bidder. He needs to stay behind bars," I protested.

"I wish it was that easy," he replied.

I swear, he looked like he had the weight of the world on his shoulders. And I'd never seen him so fearful. Those guys must have been extremely dangerous. "So, are you going to tell the senior partners what happened?" I wanted to know.

"Yes, I'm going to tell them," he assured me, and then he put his head down. I could see the shame on his face.

"What's wrong?" I asked after he lowered his head.

"I just got a lot on my mind."

I reached over to him and massaged his arm. "Well, I appreciate you calling me and allowing me to be here with you."

He lifted his head. "Thank you for coming."

Before I could utter another word, the doctor walked in the room. He was an older, slender-looking Caucasian man dressed in a long white coat, with a stethoscope draped around his neck. I stepped to the side so he could get closer to Troy.

"How you feeling?" the doctor asked.

"Not too good," Troy answered.

"So you were attacked, huh?"

"Yup. Two guys came out of nowhere."

"Did you know the guys?"

"No," Troy replied.

Hearing Troy's response made me give him a sharp look. I mean, he just told me that he knew who attacked him. And now he's singing a different tune.

"Well, I'm sure the cops will find out who did it," the doctor added as he got closer to Troy. He took the stethoscope from his neck and used it to listen to Troy's heartbeat and the functionality of his lungs. "Take a deep breath," he instructed Troy. "Take another deep breath," he instructed once more. When he was done examining Troy, he placed the stethoscope back around his neck and started another dialogue with Troy.

"So your heart and lungs sound good. The discoloration on your arms and around your torso area will go away soon. I will prescribe you a muscle relaxer and I will have one of my nurses stitch you up and then you'll be able to get out of here," he told Troy. "Do you have any questions for me?"

"No, you pretty much answered everything," Troy replied.

"Well, if you have any questions, just let your nurse know," the doctor insisted.

"Will do," Troy assured him.

As soon as the doctor left the room, I went into question mode. "Why did you tell him that you didn't know the guys that attacked you?"

"Because I can't take the chance of him telling detectives."

"Are they here?"

"No, but it wouldn't surprise me if they pop up before we get out of here. Telling them would hurt me more than help me."

I thought about what Troy had just explained and I had to agree with him. Telling the cops about who attacked him wouldn't be a good idea, so I backed off and trusted that he knew what was best for him.

The nurse came in and stitched up the open wound over his eye. After that, she handed Troy a prescription for a muscle relaxer and then she sent us on our way. I drove Troy to the pharmacy to get his medication filled. After I had his prescription in hand, I drove to his apartment. When we reached there, he called the firm, and in so many words, he told Noah what had happened, since Aaron wasn't available. He also told him that he'd work from home while he recuperated. Noah agreed.

When he finished his call with Noah, I handed him a glass of water so he could use it to take his medicine. After he took his medicine, I helped him get out of his clothes and crawl into bed. I powered on the television so that he could watch it. There was nothing entertaining to watch, so we settled on watching reruns of *M*A*S*H*. During the first commercial break, Troy sparked up another conversation about last night's dinner meeting at Aaron's home. A huge draft of anxiety engulfed me.

"I know you don't want to talk about this again, but—" he started to say, but I cut him off.

"You're right, I don't want to talk about last night. I've already told you what happened, so that's it," I spat out, and stood up from the chair next to his bed.

"So you're just going to walk out of here while I'm talking to you?"

"Look, I'm done talking about that. And if you think that I'm going to let you lie in that bed and beat me in my head with more questions, it's not going to happen. I'm going to go home before I let you give me another headache."

Troy gave me a long and hard stare. I could tell that he was getting frustrated all over again, but I couldn't care less. "What you need to do is worry about what you're going to do about your client and his bodyguards," I pointed out, and then I left the bedroom.

After I left Troy lying in bed, I strolled into the living room, sat down on the couch, and powered on the TV. Like before, nothing new was worth watching on television, so I started watching reruns of $M*A*S*H$. Before I realized it, the television started watching me, as I had dozed off and had fallen asleep. The way I found out I was asleep was when I heard Troy's voice, and that's when I opened my eyes.

"Mr. Fallen, I don't advise you to go to trial. It would be in your best interest to settle and let this thing go away quietly. Judges frown upon sexual harassment, and especially on those that have five women saying the same thing," I heard Troy say, and then I could hear crickets. I knew then that he was listening to his client's response.

"Okay, if you like, we can proceed with the deposition, but again, that may not go in your favor either. Listen, what I need you to do is sleep on what I've advised you to do. And give me a call in a couple of days. Remember, we still have time to respond," Troy added, and then he fell silent. "Sounds great, and I'll talk to you in a few days," Troy said, and then he ended his call.

I lay there and thought about the advice Troy gave to his client and immediately thought about all of the scumbags that harass and rape women in the workplace. Shit! It just happened to me. Granted, it didn't happen in the workplace by one of the partners of the firm, but it happened in their home by one of their clients. So I could only wonder if I had a sexual harassment case. But then I wondered if Aaron could get away with it, because it happened in his home and not at the office. Maybe I could sue Simon. He was very rich. And besides, I was sure he would want this to go away quietly. Allegations of sexual harassment would destroy his business. He could stand to lose a lot. So, did I have any options?

"Hi, Maggie, this is Troy, Leon's attorney. Is he available?" I heard him say. I knew then that he made another call. "Hi, Leon, how's it going?" Troy asked him. "I'm good, brother. I was calling to let you know that the DA has agreed to drop all charges if you agree to plead guilty to the wire fraud charge in exchange for one year on probation."

I couldn't hear what Leon was saying, but when Troy responded, I knew the guy was happy with the arrangement.

"Okay, great. I will have my paralegal contact the DA's Office so that we can get the ball rolling. You should hear from her in a couple of days with your final court date," Troy explained. "You do the same," he added, and then he ended the call.

Troy made another four calls to his clients, and when he ended the last call, he got up from the bed and walked into the living room, where I was. As soon as he laid eyes on me, I turned my attention toward him and waited for him to speak first.

"Hungry?"

"Yes, I am. Why? You're gonna cook something?" I asked. But I was being a smart-ass. I knew that he was in no position to cook.

He cracked a smile. "Wanna order Chinese? Pizza?"

"I would rather have pizza."

"Cool. I'll get Sal's pizza menu from the kitchen drawer if you call and place the order."

"Sure. I can do that," I agreed.

After the pizza was delivered, Troy and I helped ourselves to a large portion of it. Not much longer after that, he took another muscle relaxer and fell asleep. Poor thing, he looked really bad with the purple-and-blue discolorations, scratches, bloody wounds, and the black eye covering 80 percent of his face. I could tell that those guys meant business when they attacked him. But the messed-up part about it was that he couldn't report this incident to law enforcement for fear of his life.

Was I doing the wrong thing wanting to become an attorney? Was I going to one day represent a client that would want to hurt me if I didn't deliver what they were expecting? Maybe I needed to rethink my career field, because if I ever represented a client that wanted to kill me because I didn't win their case or get them out of jail, then I was fucked.

I watched Troy sleep, until he started snoring, and then I strolled back into the living room. I knew my mother was waiting for me to call her about Troy's condition, so to prevent waking him up, I used the telephone in the living room to make the call.

"Hi, Mom," I started off saying after she picked up.

"Hi, baby, where are you?" she didn't hesitate to ask.

"I'm at Troy's apartment."

"How is he?"

"He's banged up a bit, but the doctor gave him muscle relaxers, so he'll be fine."

"Tell me what happened?"

"He was attacked by two guys that work for one of his clients."

"No way."

"Yes. Apparently, his client wasn't satisfied with Troy's performance today in court, so he got his guys to beat him up."

"Are you pulling my leg?" my mother questioned me. I could tell that she was in disbelief.

"I wish I was, but it really happened."

"Where is Troy now?"

"He's asleep."

"Has he reported this to the police?"

"No, not yet. But he will," I lied. I knew she would beat me in my head with why it would be in his best interest to do it. I've learned through the years to tell my mother what she wanted to hear.

"Do Aaron and Noah know about this?"

"Yes, he called them as soon as we got here to his apartment."

"What did they have to say about all of this?"

"They pretty much said the same thing as you."

"He's not going to work anytime soon?"

"No, I think he's going to take a week off. Hopefully by then, the scars and discoloration around his eye will be gone."

"I swear, I don't know what this world is coming to. Who goes around and has their attorney beat up because their court case didn't go in their favor?"

"It sounds crazy, but it happened today."

"Sounds like he may need to get a bodyguard or screen his clients better."

"He may need to do both."

"Are you coming home tonight?"

"I thought about it. But Troy is going to need me to help around here. I don't have any work clothes here, so I'll stop by early tomorrow morning."

"Well, you be careful. Those guys may know where Troy lives."

"This building has a tight security team, so I doubt if they can get in here."

"Well, just be careful anyway."

"I will."

"Oh yeah, that guy Simon called here about an hour or so ago."

"What did you tell him?"

"I told him that you weren't here."

"Did you tell him where I went?"

"Of course not, what do you take me for? I told him that you had to run an errand and that I would let you know that he called."

"Thank you, Mom."

"You're welcome, darling. Now be careful and I'll see you in the morning, okay?"

"Okay."

I found something to wear the following day, so I didn't need to stop by my parents' house to get dressed. Before I left Troy, I kissed him and told him to stay in bed, and then I headed to work. As soon as I walked off the elevator, the receptionist told me to report to Aaron's office. My heartbeat sped up at that very moment. All sorts of things started running through my mind about why he wanted to see me. Knowing Aaron, I felt it could be a bevy of things. Simon could be one of them. And Troy could be the other. Then again, it could be about my job performance. Either way, I was going to have to answer questions, and it was too early in the morning for that. But I had no other choice, so there we go.

"Could you let him know that I'm on my way to his office?" I asked the receptionist.

"Absolutely," she replied, and picked up her telephone. "Mr. A., Yoshi is on her way to your office," I heard her say as I walked away from the reception desk.

Aaron's door was shut, so I knocked on it. "Come on in," he said.

When I opened his door, I found him sitting behind his desk, arranging documents scattered across it. He smiled at me and said, "Good morning."

I smiled back. "Good morning," I replied.

"Close the door and take a seat," he instructed.

"Gotcha," I said.

Immediately after I sat down, he started the dialogue. "I know you were with Troy at the hospital yesterday, and I'm glad you were. I also know that you spent the night at his apartment."

"Wait, let me explain—" I started to say, but he cut me off in midsentence.

"No, let me finish and then I'll let you talk."

"I'm sorry."

"Don't be sorry. I just want you to be aware that an intern seeing one of the partners of this firm is strictly prohibited, and it could mean immediate termination."

"I only stayed at his place so I could monitor him. I gave him his meds and I made sure that he ate. And that's all that happened."

"Listen, Yoshi, I've had my suspicions of you and Troy for a while. Now, I like you. You're a good girl and you seem really smart. So don't blow your chances of an opportunity that could benefit you for life. If you continue with a relationship with Troy, it will derail everything that you have worked so hard for. Take my advice and don't see him again outside of this firm. Do I make myself clear?" he scolded me.

Shocked and taken aback by Aaron's threats, I sat there, stunned. It was apparent that he used one of his private investigators to follow us. I wondered if Troy knew this. And I wondered if I should tell him. The audacity of this fucking old man to sit behind his desk and threaten me, and to tell me that I couldn't see Troy again, and if he found out that I was, I would get terminated. How dare he? I mean, this is the same bastard that invited me to his home and allowed a potential client to fuck me while I was intoxicated. Did he know that I would sue the fuck out of him and Simon? I swear, this old motherfucker is barking up the wrong tree.

But I was a part of his world and he was right, he could terminate me. He could even start a shitload of rumors that could prevent anyone else from hiring me. So I was going to play his game and stop seeing Troy. Well, I was going to make him think it.

"Yes, you have made it plain and clear. But can I say something?"

"Sure, go ahead."

"Troy and I are friends. He is a good guy. So, when he called me last night and told me that he needed my help, I was there."

"Was that out of obligation because of the relationship, or was it because you're a Good Samaritan?" Aaron replied sarcastically.

"Both. But if you were in that same situation, I would've come to help you as well," I insisted.

"I would never call you. I have a wife and an assistant that would help me in a time such as that."

"Well, if you did, I would help. Just like when you asked me to come to your home and help sway your client to do business with the firm. And I don't know if you know this, but when your housekeeper woke me up the following morning, I was lying underneath a bed sheet naked. Now, I don't know who removed my clothes, but it was done. I didn't say anything about it until now, but since we're on the subject about ethics and what's prohibited . . ."

"I can't believe that you don't remember doing a striptease for Simon. According to him, you took your own clothes off."

"That's a lie. I would've remembered if I had done it. And what kind of person does that make me? I'm not that type of girl. I don't do things like that," I protested in a calm manner. I wanted to curse his ass out, but I knew that he'd have my ass escorted out of this building in a heartbeat.

"So, are you saying that Simon undressed you?"

This sounded like a trick question and I didn't know how

to answer it. Do I say, *yes, I believe he did,* and then I could open the door of looking like a snitch? Not only that, Aaron would not allow me to fuck up the business relationship he had with Simon. He stood to make a bunch of money on the deal that was coming up. In addition to that, Aaron would look at me like he couldn't trust me. Like Troy said, Aaron thought of me as a liability, so I would be out of here in a hot second.

"No, I am not saying that Simon was the one that took off my clothes," I said, and then I fell silent. I knew I had to say the right words. "You know what? Forget it. It's not even that serious," I continued.

"Are you sure? The floor is yours."

"No, I've said enough. I appreciate you and Noah for allowing me to work here at this firm. It's actually an honor. So, with that said, I just want you to know that you will never have to have this conversation with me again."

Aaron smiled. "Good."

I stood up from my chair. "Thank you again, Mr. A., for this opportunity."

"You're quite welcome," he said. "Exam day is coming up," he added.

"I know. I'm a nervous wreck."

"All you got to do is study hard and you'll be fine."

"Let's hope so," I said, and then I walked out of his office.

Troy called me right before I was about to take a lunch break. The receptionist knew that it was Troy calling, so she asked me if I wanted to talk to him before transferring the call to me. "Yes, put him through," I told her.

"Working hard?" he asked me.

"Somewhat," I replied, and at the same time, I looked at Jillian through my peripheral vision. By the look on her facial expression, she knew that it was a personal call, so I told

Troy that I was about to take lunch. "Can I call you back in about ten minutes?"

"I'll be waiting for your call," he told me, and then I ended it.

From my desktop computer, I keyed in my clock-out time, and then I grabbed my handbag from the side drawer of my desk. "I'm going to take my lunch break now," I told her, and then I stood up on my feet.

"Make sure you clock out."

"I just did."

"Okay. See you back in an hour."

"See you then," I replied, and then I strolled out of the office.

I had no idea what I wanted for lunch. I just wanted to get out of this building before I ripped out all of my hair. As soon as I exited the building, I walked a block up the street and went to a café. The waitress behind the counter told me that I could sit anywhere I wanted and that she'd be over to take my order.

"Do you guys have a phone booth in here?" I asked her. I could use my own cellphone but it was given to me by the firm and I don't want my call log monitored by Aaron or Noah.

"Yes, it's in the back, where the restrooms are," the middle-aged Caucasian woman said.

I thanked her and headed in the direction she instructed me to go. The pay phone was exactly where she said it was. I grabbed a quarter from my purse, pushed it in the change slot, and then I dialed Troy's phone number. He answered on the second ring.

"Hello," he said.

"It's me."

"Where are you?"

"At a diner a block from the firm."

"What are you going to have for lunch?"

"I really don't have an appetite. Aaron took that away when he cornered me in his office and threatened to terminate me if I continue seeing you."

"No fucking way. He said that to you?" Troy asked as the volume of his voice escalated.

"Yes, he did."

"What brought on that conversation with you and him?"

"Besides the fact that he witnessed you yelling at me in the conference room at the firm, he knew that I went to the hospital to see you, and he knew that I took you home. He even knew that I spent the night with you last night. He said that he knew that you and I have been an item for a while now. And he said that it's not a good look that an intern is seeing a partner in the firm. He acted like he wanted to fire me today, but I told him that it wouldn't happen again."

"You should've pleaded the Fifth."

"We are not in court. And besides, he's got one of the private investigators watching us. I just know it. I mean, how else did he know that I spent the night at your apartment and left this morning?"

"He's already brought it to my attention. He told me to leave you alone, and I promised him that I would, so why is he going behind my back and questioning you?" Troy became angry.

"What are we going to do? He said that I can't see you anymore."

"Fuck that! He can't tell me what woman I'm allowed to be with. Don't worry, I'm going to handle it."

"I don't think that'll be a good idea, Troy. He threatened to fire me."

"So, what do you want me to do? Just sit back and let him run our lives?"

"Don't act like you've been peaches and cream either. The way you treated me those two times was horrifying."

"That's because I don't want to think about another man touching you. It drives me crazy."

"You just need to see a shrink or something. That other side of you is not pretty."

"So, what now?" he wanted to know.

"I think that we should lay low for a couple of weeks. And whoever he has following us will see that we're not spending time together and then they'll fall back."

"That fucking piece of shit probably wants to fuck you and that's why he wants to cock-block me. And then to talk down to you has my blood boiling."

"Well, what can we do about it? He's adamant about us not seeing each other anymore."

"That son of a bitch! Did you know that he met his wife at the firm? She already had a husband and he broke up their happy home. The fucking husband held Aaron at gunpoint and almost took his fucking life. He would be dead now if one of the other partners hadn't saved him."

"How long ago was this?" I wondered aloud.

"Over twenty years ago. And that's not it, that sick son of a bitch fucked one of our secretaries when I was first hired, and when she wanted to stop the affair, he fired her. So, how dare he put stipulations on someone else's relationship?"

"Did his wife know about the affair with the secretary?"

"No, but she would've found out if the young lady hadn't called off the affair."

"He is such a hypocrite."

"Yeah, he is. And do you see why I was acting the way I was when I found out that you went to his home alone? It's all about sex with those guys. They figure if they throw their weight around, show women how much money and power they have, and then they can pull them into their web of lies and dominate them with control. He and his whole club of good ol' boys."

"Club?"

"You're fucking right it is. I begged to join because of the good things they do for the inner-city kids and the fund-raising campaigns they put together to help people diagnosed with cancer. And if you're in this club, you also get special treatment around town. Everywhere any of the members go, they get VIP treatment. If you get into a little trouble, you have judges that would dismiss all charges. You can literally get in places that are at full capacity. It's like a young guy's dream to be connected on that level. But after joining, I saw how things really happen behind the scenes, and I regret being initiated to this very day."

"What goes on behind the scenes?" I wanted to know. From everything Troy was telling me, it sounded like he was mixed up in some kind of cult.

"Secret meetings. . . . You name it, it goes on at the bottom floor of this building."

"You mean like some Illuminati type of shit?"

Troy fell silent. He did not respond to my question for some reason. "Troy, are you up here?" I asked him.

But he didn't utter one word. "Baby, are you up here?" I asked again.

"Yes, I'm up here. But did you hear that clicking sound?" he asked.

"No. I didn't. When did it happen?"

"Just a few seconds ago. I heard it twice."

"No, I didn't hear it."

"Oh shit! They tapped my phone. Maybe the whole apartment."

"Who?"

"The people I work for. And this isn't my first time hearing it. I heard it a few times on my car phone."

"Oh my God! You might be right," I started off saying. "That's probably why Aaron knew that I picked you up at the hospital and spent the night at your apartment," I continued, and then I paused so that Troy could add to the conversation. But once again, he wouldn't talk.

"Hello," I said.

"I'm here," he finally said. "Hey, I've gotta go. I'll talk to you later," he added, and then the phone line went dead. Puzzled by his actions, I wanted to call him back, but I knew that it wouldn't be a good idea, because maybe his phones were tapped. And what did that mean for us? If this was, in fact, true, then the senior partners at the firm could monitor our communication for sure.

8

Troy

If my phones were tapped, someone was going to answer to me, because this was unlawful and an invasion of my privacy. Aaron was the first person on my list to call because he had some explaining to do. "Aaron, we need to have a talk," I didn't hesitate to say after he picked up his phone.

"Oh, Troy, what's going on? Are you feeling better?" Aaron asked me in a cheerful manner. He and I both knew that he was full of shit.

"Do you guys have my phones tapped? My house bugged?"

"Phones tapped? Bugging your home?" Aaron wanted clarity.

"Yes, *bugged*, *tapped*, all of it means the same," I said irritably.

"Of course not. What would make you say something as foolish as that? I'm not an officer of the law, I am an officer of the courts, and it's against the law to do that sort of thing."

"Every time I'm on a call, I hear a clicking sound in the background. I've even heard my voice echo a few times."

He chuckled. "Stop being paranoid. No one has tapped your telephones or bugged your place," he insisted.

"What's this I hear about you threatening to fire Yoshi? And tell me how you knew that she picked me up from the hospital and spent the night at my apartment?"

"Oh, so she's talked to you, huh?"

"Yes, she called and told me that we had to cut off all communication."

"Smart girl."

"How dare you tell her that she can't see me again?"

"Troy, I did you a favor."

"How is that?"

"She's damaged goods. Did she tell you that she slept with Simon?"

Instantly angered by Aaron's words, I knew my eyes turned red. "That's a lie!" I roared. But deep down inside, I knew it to be true. I felt it in my bones the moment I found out that Simon signed on to have the firm represent him. Not only that, Aaron and Noah both always picked out women from the firm that he could pimp out to potential new clients. That was his MO.

"No, it's not a lie, and you of all people know that. Didn't I tell you to leave her alone because she was a liability?"

"Yes, but you already knew that I was seeing her, and that's why you pulled me into your office."

"It sounds like you have feelings for her?"

"I care for her a little."

"She's not right for you. She's not the one you could take home to your parents. What would they have said if you brought a black woman home to meet them? You're supposed to date and court women from the same pedigree as you. You're wasting your time, son. Move on."

"Aaron, she's different."

"Yes, she is. She's even beautiful. But she is not a trophy wife. She is not the one you wanna have children with. By all means, have sex with her. But I don't think that you should be seen with her in public. You've got a clean imagine. Don't tarnish it by walking around holding hands with a black woman at black-tie affairs and fund-raisers. Our wealthy counterparts and peers will frown upon that and we'll end up with no money by the end of the night. Do you get where I am coming from, son?"

I knew where Aaron was coming from because of the older and conservative men he rubbed elbows with, but I was not a part of that club. I was different. I was cut from a different cloth. My parents didn't raise me to be stuffy prestigious. So, how should I handle this situation?

"Yes, I get where you're coming from," I finally answered him, even though I wanted to tell him to *go and fuck off*.

"How are you feeling? You know with the injuries and such?" Aaron changed the subject.

"I'm feeling a little better," I forced myself to say. I was still steaming from hearing that Yoshi fucked Simon. I just couldn't shut those emotions off by allowing someone to change the subject.

"Don't get addicted to those prescription meds," Aaron said jokingly. "I was wondering," he said, and then fell silent for a moment. "Do you think it would be wise to get yourself security?"

"I thought about it. But then I figured that what happened to me with those guys was an isolated incident, so why walk around with a bodyguard? I would be the laughingstock of the courts."

"Yes, you're probably right. We don't want to send out a wrong message. Having a bodyguard could paint the picture that it's not safe to be in your presence, and what potentially happens to you could indeed happen to your clients."

"While I'm home, I will mull over everything and get back to you after I figure things out."

"So, is Mr. Fallen set on doing his deposition?"

"He is. But I'm trying to prevent him from doing it. The plaintiff has a strong case and she will bury him publicly if he pushes the envelope."

"Yes, I agree. I'm going to give him a call later because it sounds like he needs to hear a voice of reason."

"Yeah, he does."

"Okay, well, I'm going to have lunch now."

"All right. I'll wait to hear from you later."

"Sounds good," Aaron said, and then I ended our call.

That fucking bitch! I knew it. I knew she fucked Simon. But she lied to me. She swore that it didn't happen, but I knew in my gut that it did. I knew the type of men I worked around. I knew that they were snakes and vultures. They would eat your children if you allowed them. That fucking whore! I was going to kill her, I swear, when I got my fucking hands on her. Ugh!!!!

Not being able to call her back angered me. I wanted to talk to her now. She had some explaining to do. And if she started lying, there was a large percentage that I might choke her because I loved her. I really had deep feelings for Yoshi. I didn't care if she was black. She meant a lot to me. So to know that another man touched her in that way was damaging my heart right now. I knew one thing, if the rib area of my chest and stomach weren't in pain, I would fuck him up. He was a weak old man and I could easily take that asshole down. I knew that I'd be terminated from the firm on the spot, and I was sure Simon would have me arrested. So, how would I make this pain go away? I needed to get rid of it. And get rid of it now.

9

Yoshi

After I got off the phone with Troy, I grabbed a BLT and a can of Sprite from the café and ate it while I walked back to the firm. The second I stepped on the elevator, I shoved the rest of my sandwich into my mouth. When the elevator door opened, I drank the last bit of soda I had left in the can and then I stepped off the elevator.

The receptionist turned in my direction and smiled. Her eyes lit up. "I just called your desk," she said.

I smiled back, curious as to why her face was beaming. "What's going on?" I wanted to know.

She turned her attention to a vase placed on the edge of her desk filled with two dozen roses. "Those were just delivered about three minutes ago," she told me.

"By who?" I asked as I walked toward the vase.

"The driver from the florist shop down the block," she replied.

I smelled the roses and they smelled lovely. I didn't have to pull the card buried in the middle to know that they came from Simon.

"They smell good, huh?" she commented.

"Yes, they do." I agreed. "Can you throw this away?" I added, and handed her my empty can of Sprite.

"Sure," she said.

After I passed her the can, I picked up the vase filled with roses and carried them to the office I shared with Jillian. As I walked in, I got Jillian's attention. She immediately rolled her eyes and turned her focus back to her desktop computer. I shook my head with disappointment. She made it painfully obvious how jealous she was about my gift. I politely placed the vase on my desk, and then I took the card sent with the roses and started reading it: *Just a note to let you know that I've been thinking about you. Enjoy your day!*

"Have you clocked back in the system?" Jillian asked abruptly.

I turned my attention toward her. "I still have two minutes left," I replied sarcastically.

Instead of commenting, she sucked her teeth and rolled her eyes, finally turning her attention back to her computer monitor.

I wanted to burst into laughter, but I knew that it wouldn't end well. This woman had it out for me, and she was making it blatantly clear how much she disliked me. I swear, I couldn't wait to get out of here today. Everyone had been chewing my ass out. First it was Aaron and now Jillian. Well, let me correct that, because Jillian was always on my back. She was one miserable bitch.

As soon as my lunchtime ended, I clocked back in, and immediately after I had done so, Jillian clocked out and took her lunch break. It was such a great feeling to see her ass go. I got tired of sitting underneath the black cloud she had created and was now hanging above our heads. I would do anything to share an office with someone else in the firm. This bitch was unbearable and I needed an outlet before I lost my cool. But then again, I figured, who was I? The meeting I had with Aaron hadn't gone in my favor, so if I complained about my working environment with Jillian, he'd probably laugh me out of his office. So, for now, all I could do was grin and bear it.

For some reason, my day at work seemed like it took forever. Instead of doing an eight-hour shift, it seemed like I was there for fifteen hours. The environment was that brutal. So, as soon as I exited the building with the vase in hand, I took a deep breath and exhaled.

"Finally," I uttered from my lips as the mild breeze brushed my face.

"What the fuck you mean, *finally*?" I heard a voice behind me say. Startled, I looked over my shoulders. It was Troy walking behind me in the parking garage. It seemed as though he was hiding behind a nearby car.

I covered my chest area with my hand. "You scared me."

"So I take it that Simon bought you those motherfucking flowers?" he growled, wearing a pair of shades to cover up the black eye he got the previous day. Before I was able to reply, he lunged back and delivered a mighty blow with his fist. The glass vase fell to the ground and shattered into many pieces. The flowers and water sat in the thick of it.

"What is wrong with you?" I shouted.

"You lied to me!" he roared, and grabbed ahold of my neck and started squeezing it as hard as he could. I started coughing and gagging as I struggled to get his hand from around my neck.

"I can't breathe," I finally managed to say between each cough.

By this time, he pushed me back against a nearby car and the car alarm instantly started blaring. The noise was loud and piercing, and the millisecond that Troy turned his attention to the alarm gave me the window to break away from him. And that's what I did. I pushed him backward and made a run to my car. He was on my heels, but, thankfully, I had my keys in hand and was able to get into my car before he got within five feet of me. I immediately locked the door and started up the engine.

He was livid and stood behind my car so that I couldn't back up. "Move out of my way, Troy!" I shouted while the alarm from the other car continued to go off. The noise alone was driving me crazy.

"No, you are going to talk to me right now," he yelled over the piercing noise coming from the car alarm.

I put my car in reverse to back up, but Troy wouldn't budge. I even put my feet on the brake and eased off it, with every inch I took, to see if he would move and he didn't. "What are you going to do, back into me?" he shouted.

"Troy, move out of my way!" I screamed. I was over it. He had pushed my last button. I mean, how dare he put his fucking hands on me? My heart was literally starting to throb with pain.

While I was trying to get Troy out of the way, the owner of the vehicle came down to the garage and turned off the alarm. It was a white guy, dressed in an expensive suit, whom I had seen before, while riding the elevator. I think he worked for the marketing firm two floors down from the law firm. I saw him walk up to Troy and utter a few words. Having him interact with Troy gave me another window of opportunity to get away from him.

"Excuse me," I shouted while looking through my rearview mirror. The white guy moved to the side. Troy reluctantly followed suit with the other guy.

The guy carried on a conversation with Troy as I eased out of the parking spot. "Thank you," I said to them both. The white guy said, "You're welcome," while Troy stared me down in the black sunglasses. As I drove in reverse, I heard the guy ask Troy whose broken vase and flowers were there. I didn't hear Troy's response, but I'm more than sure that he lied about it. Probably told the guy that they were there when he and I walked into the parking garage.

Once I was out on the streets of New York, I put the pedal to the metal and drove home without incident. Okay, I drove over the speed limit the entire way, but I didn't get any driver infractions, so I was good to go.

When I walked into the front door, my stepfather was there watching television in the TV room and my mother was nowhere in sight. I dropped my purse on the floor next to the sofa and collapsed down, like I was out of energy.

"How was your day?" he started off the conversation.

I took a deep breath and then exhaled. "Long. But I managed to get through it," I said. "Where is Mom?" I wondered aloud.

"She said she had a hair appointment."

"How long has she been gone?"

"She left around two p.m., so she should be on her way home."

"How has your day been?" I wanted to know.

"I played golf. Had lunch at the country club. So it's been eventful."

"Win any games?"

"A couple. But I don't go out there to win games. I just need an outlet, and that's what golf does for me."

"What did you have for lunch?"

"Grilled chicken Caesar salad, and it was delicious."

"What did you have to drink?"

"Club soda."

"Why not scotch or vodka?"

"I drink enough of that here," he commented, and then he chuckled. "So, are you still studying for your bar exam?" he added.

"I get asked that same question every day, it seems like."

"Well, are you?"

"Of course, I am. With the amount of pressure I have on me to pass, I have no other alternative but study every chance I get."

"Have you decided to stay at the firm you're at? Or work for another one? Because the Weinstein brothers are a big deal in New York. They are both brilliant attorneys and they know a lot of people that could open doors for you all over the country," he boasted.

"Do you know them on a personal level?"

"Yes, I used them when I divorced the woman before your mother. And I came out on top. Your mother has used them for other things. So, yes, I know them on a personal level. Why do you ask?"

"Because I don't like some of the stuff that goes on around there. Aaron's and Noah's paralegal, Jillian, is a bitch. The men around there think that they are superior. I swear, I can go on and on about them. Now, don't get me wrong, I am grateful for the opportunity that they're giving me, but I don't think that's somewhere I want to work permanently."

"Don't tell your mother that. She'll have a fit."

"Trust me, I won't."

"So, where would you go?"

"You mean firm or state?" I let out a long sigh. "I'm thinking about checking out Miami. You know, see what they have to offer."

"Why so far?"

"I have a friend whom I went to ODU with. Her name is Maria. She studied law too. She's down there and she loves it."

"Sounds exciting."

"Yeah, it does, doesn't it?"

While my stepfather and I chopped it up about my future plans, post passing the bar exam, the telephone started ringing.

"You can get that if you want," he mentioned as he glanced at the telephone placed next to the lamp on the end table near the sofa.

"Where is the housekeeper?" I asked him while dreading answering it myself. The thought of me answering it, and it being Troy, wasn't what I wanted to do.

"She left for the day," he replied after the phone rang for the second time. "You don't want to answer it?" he wondered aloud.

"No, I don't. So, will you please answer it?" I asked nicely. He smiled. "Sure," he said.

I handed him the telephone. "If it's Troy, tell him I'm not here," I instructed him.

He winked his eye. "Hello," he said to the caller.

Of course, I couldn't hear the caller, but when my stepfather looked at me, I knew it was Troy. Damn, it felt good to have dodged that bullet.

"And you are?" my stepfather said. "Hold on, let me see if she's available," my stepfather continued.

"It's Simon," he whispered while muffling the receiver end of the phone with his hands.

I hesitated for a second, wondering if I should take Simon's call. I knew that he was calling to find out if I received the roses, considering I hadn't called him to say thank you. Even then, my mind was too clouded with the drama I had with Troy earlier to get on a call and give Simon my full attention, so I motioned for my stepfather to tell him that I wasn't available.

"Tell him I'm in the shower," I whispered.

"Hi, Simon, she's taking a shower right now. Can I have her call you back?" my stepfather asked him. "Okay, will do," he added, and then he hung up the call.

He handed me the telephone to put back on the lamp table. "Who is Simon?" he asked. I could see his curiosity was piqued.

"Nobody," I replied nonchalantly, because in my mind, Simon was just that, a nobody. Anyone that lied and told me that I knew that I'd consented to having sex with him the other night, while I was under the influence, was straight bullshit. I'd never *not* remembered whom I fucked.

"I'm sorry, but if he's breathing, then he is a somebody."

"He's a new client that just signed on to be repped by the firm. I met him at the dinner meeting at Aaron's penthouse the other night."

"So, why is he calling you?"

"Because he likes me."

"How old is he?"

"Fifty, maybe."

"Wow! That's a bit old for you."

"I said the same thing."

"Isn't it against a certain code of ethics at the firm? Employees aren't permitted to socialize with clients?"

"Yes."

"Does he know that?"

"I'm sure he does."

"You know I don't meddle in your personal life, but I will say, *please be careful*. Getting involved with an older man doesn't end well."

"Dealing with much younger guys doesn't end well either," I commented.

"Care to share?"

"Not really."

"Well, if you need to talk, I'm always here."

"I know you are, and that's why I love you so much," I told him, and then I stood up from the sofa. I grabbed my purse, kissed my stepfather on the cheek, and headed into my bedroom, but before I could get through the entryway of my bedroom, there was a knock on the front door. "Could you see who that is?" I peered back in the TV room and asked.

"Sure," my stepfather agreed.

I heard movement from him as he stood up from his recliner. I waited for him to come in the hallway, where I was, because I suspected that the person at the front door could possibly be Troy. And as he passed me, I gave him instructions.

"If it's Troy, I am not here," I told him, and then I entered my bedroom. I closed my bedroom door, but I left it slightly ajar to hear what was about to happen.

"Who is it?" he asked.

"It's your wife. Open this door," I heard my mother say.

My dad opened the door. "Where is your key?"

"In the bottom of my purse. I just got my nails done and I didn't want to smear the polish."

"I offered to get them from her purse, but she wasn't having it," I heard another voice say. And within a couple of seconds, I knew it was Troy. My heart dropped into the pit of my stomach.

"Oh no, I won't have it. Tell 'em, honey, I don't let no man go in my purse. That's how I was raised. My mother taught me that," my mother replied.

"Yeah, she's right. No one goes into her purse, but her," my stepfather agreed, and then I heard the front door close.

"Hi, Troy, what brings you here?" my stepfather added.

"Came by to talk to your daughter," he announced.

"Yeah, where is she?" my mother chimed in.

"She's in her bedroom," my stepfather told her.

I heard my mother's footsteps as they got closer to my bedroom. I closed the door completely shut and then I sat down on the edge of my bed.

She knocked on the door. "Come in," I said in a low tone so that only she could hear me.

She opened my bedroom door and walked in. "What's wrong with you? And why are you looking like that?"

"Close the door," I instructed her.

After she closed it, she approached me. "You know, Troy is in the foyer with your stepfather. He wants to see you."

"Tell 'em, I'm taking a nap or something."

My mother took a seat next to me. "What's wrong, darling?"

"He found out about the roses that Simon sent me."

"How did he find out?"

"I'm not talking about those. He had another arrangement sent to the office, so when I got off, I grabbed them so I could bring them home. But while I was walking to my car, he came from out of nowhere, saw the roses, and went crazy. He knocked them out of my hands and started going ballistic."

"Did he put his hands on you?"

I was about to tell her that he did, in fact, put his hands on me. But I knew that she would storm out of my room and confront Troy about it. She might even hit him—who knows?—but the situation would only escalate.

"No, Mom, he didn't," I lied.

"Did he disrespect you? Call you out of your name?"

"No," I said, lying to her once more. See again, if you're not sure that you're done with your significant other, don't tell your loved ones how badly you think they are treating you. Because they will build a wall of hate and they will never like that person again. You might even have to choose between that person and the ones that love you.

"Well, what did he say?"

"Just some mean stuff," I finally said. "Tell 'em that I don't want to see him right now, and when I'm ready to talk, I will call him."

"Okay. You got it," she said, and then she stood up from my bed.

When she exited my bedroom, she closed the door behind her, but I opened it and had it slightly ajar so I could hear her tell Troy to leave.

"Troy, honey, Yoshi said that she doesn't want to talk right now. But she will call you later," my mother said.

"No, no, no, Mrs. Lomax, I need to talk to her now," Troy protested.

"Well, that's not going to happen. She was very adamant when she told me to tell you that she doesn't want to talk to you right now. So you're going to have to wait until she's ready."

"I'm sorry, Mrs. Lomax, no disrespect, but I'm not leaving here until I see and talk to her."

"Oh no, son. You're going to leave now. And if you don't leave willingly, I'm going to put you out," my stepfather threatened him.

Now there I was, standing by my bedroom door, listening to Troy tell my parents that he was not leaving their apartment until he spoke with me. Now I hadn't been knowing Troy for a long time, but I knew when he was sincere about something. Judging from the tone of his voice, he seemed desperate, so I believed him when he said that he wasn't leaving until he saw me. My parents are much older people, and their health is not in tip-top shape, so with one blow from Troy, he could potentially hurt my stepdad. My mother's state of physicality was much worse. I didn't think that she'd ever been in a fight, so he'd probably knock her out in one blow, and I couldn't allow that to happen. My best option was to let this guy see me before it got ugly in this house.

Without thinking about it any further, I exited my bedroom and headed toward the foyer. When I turned the corner, I saw my stepfather position himself to grab Troy. Thank God I caught him in time before he touched Troy. "Mom, Dad, I got it," I told them.

Troy let out an expression of relief and satisfaction. He turned toward me, like I was the only person in the room. He instantly started apologizing. "I am so sorry. Please let's talk about this," he started begging and pleading with me.

My mother and stepfather stood on the sidelines and watched Troy as he engaged me. It was like he was showing a different side of himself.

"Are you all right being around this guy?" my stepfather asked me. He gave me a look of concern.

"I think you should be more concerned about your daughter allowing a complete stranger to screw her brains out," Troy mentioned. And, I swear, the entire house went radio silent.

"What did you just say?" my mother asked him. I could tell that she was about to unleash her wrath on him.

"Yoshi didn't tell you guys?" Troy asked them.

"Troy, you are out of line," I hissed. My heart rate started picking up traction.

"Yeah, what did you just say?" my stepfather interjected.

"She allowed a man she just met at Aaron's penthouse apartment the other night to bang her brains out," Troy stated in a deceitful manner.

"I don't believe that nonsense," my mother hissed.

"And neither do I." My stepfather joined forces with my mother.

"Tell them, Yoshi. Tell your parents how you allowed the firm's new client to screw your brains out." He was pressuring me. He wouldn't take his eyes off me. My mother and stepfather waited for my answer too.

"He's lying," I finally said. I mustered up the most sincere expression and lied to them. There was no way I could tell them what had happened at Aaron's place the other night. They would be brokenhearted.

"You are such a fucking liar!" Troy roared. He acted like he wanted to attack me. My stepfather noticed it and stepped up to him.

"You disrespectful piece of shit. Get out of my house right now!" my stepfather barked.

"Yes, you heard my husband, get out of our house," my mother chimed in.

"I'm not going anywhere, unless Yoshi goes too," he bargained.

"Yoshi isn't going anywhere with you," both my parents said.

"It's gonna get really ugly in here if she doesn't leave with me," Troy threatened.

"Do you know what I would do to you, young man?" my stepfather warned him.

"You will do no such thing," Troy assured him.

"Yoshi call the cops on this joker! Telling me and my husband that he's not leaving our home. He must be crazy!" my mother shouted.

"It's okay, you guys. I'll handle it," I finally broke down and said. I didn't want my parents getting into a scuffle with Troy. My stepfather was a big guy, but he just had hip surgery. I couldn't have him risking himself to prove that he's our protector.

"No, Yoshi. This guy is dangerous. What kind of father would I be to let you go alone with this guy after he threatened to hurt us?"

"I'm gonna call Aaron and Noah. They'll straighten this whole thing out," my mother announced, and then she walked

away from the circle we formed during this chaotic engagement.

"Mom, I told you guys, I've got it."

"Nope, I'm not listening to you. I'm calling Aaron right
now," she insisted.

I grabbed her arm and stopped her before she could walk
off. "I've got it, Mom," I assured her, and after standing
there for a total of three seconds, she said, "Okay, but he has
to leave our apartment now."

I released her arm and then I looked at Troy, who was already staring me down. "Let's go, Troy."

"Are you coming with me?" he wanted to know.

I reluctantly said yes and my parents instantly expressed
their concern for me. "If he touches you, I will be forced to
thrash him and drag him out of this building," my stepfather
stated.

"Let me just do it my way, guys. Nothing will happen. I
promise," I lied once more.

I was honestly in limbo about what was going to happen
to me, once I was alone with Troy. I didn't know if he was
going to fly off the handle again. I was clueless. But I knew
that it wouldn't be wise to continue to allow Troy in their
space any longer. They were already upset by the way he was
disrespecting me and them. Not to mention the allegation
that I slept with Simon. My mother was floored when those
words spewed from Troy's mouth. I knew that when all of
this was over, she would be addressing that claim to me pri-
vately.

"Let's go," I instructed Troy, and then I held out my hand,
insisting that he walk toward the front door and that I would
follow.

Thankfully, he took that direction very well, because he
started walking toward the front door without saying another word. And when he realized that I was going to meet

with him alone, his whole tune changed. He stopped at the door and then turned around and looked at both of my parents. "I'm sorry, Mrs. Lomax. I said some pretty messed-up things to you guys and Yoshi, and all I wanted to do was apologize, that's all."

"You're wasting your breath if you think I want to hear an apology right now," my mother said.

"Yes, I don't want to hear that mess either," my stepfather agreed.

"I'm sorry that you feel that way," he added.

"Leave it alone. You've said enough," I said.

"Are you sure you wanna be alone with this maniac?" my stepfather asked me as he and my mother stood next to each other.

"Yes, I will be fine," I said. But once again, I hadn't the foggiest idea. All I could do was play this whole thing by ear.

"I think you should take him down to the lobby. I don't want any of my next-door neighbors hearing you guys talking about your issues," my mother stated.

"I know, Mommy. I know," I agreed, and then Troy and I exited my parents' apartment.

After I closed the front door, I escorted Troy to the elevator and pressed the button. While we waited for it to stop on our floor, I got in his face and vented my frustrations with him. "You got a lot of fucking balls showing up at my parents' house telling them that I fucked Simon. What is your problem? Do you know how that accusation affected my mother? You were so fucking out of line! And then to act like you were going to start a war if I didn't come with you. You're nuts!"

"I did it because I knew this would be the only way I could get your attention," he summarized his behavior.

Before I could give him a rebuttal, the elevator door

opened and a resident from the upper floor was already inside. We spoke to her and remained quiet the entire ride to the first floor. But as soon as the elevator door opened, Troy let the lady go first, I stepped off after her, and then he followed me. I decided that it was best if we went into the workout area of the building. No one ever went there this time of the day. The residents in this building only work out in the morning, very late at night, or on the weekends.

I escorted him over to a set of benches near the weights area of the gym. I took a seat on one of them and he sat down on the other one and faced me. "My parents aren't gonna allow you to come to their place anymore."

"I don't care about that."

"Well, I do. And besides, that part about me fucking Simon was humiliating. You tried to paint me as a whore in front of my parents. That was fucked up, Troy."

"Aaron told me point blank that you slept with Simon," he came straight out and said it.

"I don't believe this."

"What don't you believe? The fact that you did? Or the fact that Aaron told me?" Troy asked mildly. But I could sense that he was getting irritated by the second.

"It's taking a lot of wheel power for me to sit here and give you explanations about what I did and didn't do. I don't owe you anything. You threw my respect for you out the window when you put your hands on me, and when you told my parents that I fucked Simon. It was foul and blatant and I am disgusted."

"How do you think I feel knowing that a woman I love slept with another man?"

"Troy, I didn't sleep with Simon," I replied as sincerely as I could.

"Yoshi, Aaron wouldn't lie to me about something like

that. Just be honest about it and tell me the truth," he began to plead.

I immediately thought for a second, and then I said, "If I tell you something, you promise not to fly off the handle?"

"Are you going to tell me the truth?" he asked, and then he leaned forward in my direction.

"Yes."

"Well, I'm all ears."

"Simon raped me," I finally admitted.

And when the words left my mouth, it seemed like a huge weight lifted from my shoulders. But that same level of weight looked like it transferred over to Troy. I watched in what seemed like slow motion how his energy changed. His facial expression went from calm to menacing. He rose up on his feet and picked up a ten-pound weight within reach and slung it across the room, almost hitting the glass-encased wall that wrapped around this area. I watched in horror as he turned his attention back toward me and started throwing blows in the air like someone was standing there. Saliva started drooling from his mouth as well.

"I am going to fucking kill him!" Troy roared. "I am going to take his fucking life!" he threatened.

I got up from the bench and moved backward so that he didn't make the mistake of hitting me. But I did say a few words, hoping that he'd calm down. "Troy, please stop. You're scaring me," I said softly.

"Yoshi, I am going to kill that fucking guy. I swear, he dies tonight," he warned me. By this time, his sunglasses had fallen off his face.

"Please calm down, Troy. There are security cameras in here," I told him.

And with that bit of information, he calmed down a little. He walked over to the glass-encased wall and looked out of it, like he was waiting for someone to walk by. But what he was really doing was looking at his reflection in the glass.

"I can't believe that grimy motherfucker raped you," he mumbled, and then he pressed both of his hands against his ears and started squeezing his head like someone would do to deflate a basketball. Then he growled like a dog. He was scaring me all over again.

"Troy, please stop it. You're scaring me," I begged him. My heart was beating uncontrollably.

After a couple of seconds, he dropped his arms down to his side and turned around to face me. This time, his eyes were watery and I didn't know whether to embrace him or stay where I was.

"You know the worst thing that could happen to a man is when he finds out that another man raped his woman. That's the worst feeling in the world. I mean, it's worse than if I found out that you had an affair," he started explaining.

I didn't know how to respond, so I just stood there.

"Yoshi, I feel so fucking defeated standing right here. I feel powerless and I feel weak. And those are the worst feelings to get rid of."

"And that's why I didn't want to tell you."

"That wouldn't have worked either. I would've found out eventually, and there's no telling how I would've reacted."

"But look at you. You're a walking, ticking time bomb."

Troy grabbed his shades from the floor and sat back down on the bench. "Sit down and tell me what happened," he said.

I sat back down and immediately dug deep down inside of me, trying to figure out a way to tell him exactly what happened without further making him feel like shit. Simon had already crushed Troy's heart and ego by sleeping with me, so I knew it was important for me to choose my words carefully to avoid any more of Troy's outbursts or, worse, storming out of there to go and look for Simon and do something that he couldn't come back from.

"I'm waiting," he reminded me.

I took a deep breath and sighed. "When I arrived at Aaron's penthouse, Simon was already there. He and Aaron were in the cigar lounge area, smoking. We all talked. We ate. As time wound down, Aaron excused himself and left Simon and me in the room. We talked more. We drank more, and then everything went dark. I swear, I didn't remember anything after that. But when I woke up the next morning in one of Aaron's guest bedrooms, I knew that something happened. When I looked between my legs, I was all wet."

"So you're telling me that you didn't remember anything?"

"No, I didn't."

"So, how is that you don't remember anything, but you know that Simon raped you?"

"Because when the housekeeper woke me up, I was completely naked. And later, when I asked Simon had he had his way with me, his response was like, *You don't remember? We had a wonderful night.*"

"He's only saying that to protect his ass. Did you tell Aaron about it?"

"Yes, I spoke with him about it earlier, when he threatened to fire me if I continued to see you. So I was like, *So it's okay to have a client sleep with me but it's against company policy not to see someone you're working with?*"

"What did he say?"

"I really don't remember. I pretty much checked out of the conversation after he told me to stop seeing you," I lied. I wasn't in the mood to rehash that conversation I had with Aaron about Simon.

"I want you to file rape charges against Simon."

"What?!" I asked him.

"I want you to go down to the DA's Office and file rape charges against Simon. But you're going to have to go to the emergency room to take a rape kit first."

"Troy, this happened two nights ago. If I was going to do that, then I should've done it back then."

"What about the panties you were wearing that night? A doctor can extract DNA from them."

"Troy, you are not hearing me. I am not filing charges against Simon. Do you know what would happen to me? Aaron would testify on Simon's behalf and make it look like I was a tramp. Then he would blackball me. Have my name and face on the front page of the *New York Times*. And do you know what that would do to my parents? It would crush my mother's poor heart. Everywhere she goes, someone would taunt her behind my rape scandal. And I wouldn't be able to live with myself if that happened. So, no, I am not doing it."

"You know what, I can see right through this shit. It's not about your mother or you being blackballed. It's about you liking Simon. I mean, who would accept fucking roses from a man who they claimed raped them? I wouldn't, so all of that bullshit about you drank too much, and he took advantage of you, is all a lie. You consented to fucking him and that's why you're refusing to put him in jail. So you know what? Fuck you!" he spat out, and stood up on his feet. "I hope the next time you suck his dick, you choke on it," he added, and then stormed out of the gym.

At one point, I thought he was going to hit me. But thank God he didn't. And whether or not he believed me didn't faze me at this point. I told him the truth, and that was all I could do. Who knows? Maybe he'd believe later on that it happened. But by then, it would be too late, because I'd now decided that it would be best for me to relocate to Miami.

But wait, I realized I couldn't pass my bar exam here and expect to use it in Florida. If I wanted to practice law in Florida, I was going to have to take their bar exam. Well, I guess it was time to put in my two weeks' notice.

*   *   *

When I returned to my parents' apartment, they were both in the kitchen discussing what they should eat for dinner.

"Honey, is that you?" my mother asked after she heard the front door open and close.

"Yes, it's me," I replied, and made my way into the kitchen.

"Where is Troy? Is he still here?" she wanted to know.

"No, he's gone."

"Thank God!" she added.

"You do know that I was about to break that guy in half. Coming in my house, telling my wife that he wasn't leaving," my stepfather said.

"What was his deal? And why was he wearing sunglasses in my home?" my mother wanted to know.

"I told you that he was attacked yesterday. He's got a black eye underneath those glasses."

"They must've beat him up pretty bad," my stepfather commented.

"They did," I told him.

"Well, good. That's what he gets. I'm sure he deserved every punch they threw at him," my mother commented.

"How did that whole thing start with him accusing you of sleeping with that guy?" my stepfather asked me.

"When I was leaving work earlier, he saw me carrying a vase full of roses and immediately became upset. He knocked them out of my hand and the vase shattered on the ground."

"You do know that if a man shows that level of anger, he will eventually put his hands on you. You better watch that guy, because something tells me that he's bad news. And the way he talked to your mother was very disrespectful," my stepfather insisted.

"Yes."

"Was it true about what he said? You sleeping with that guy Simon?" my mother questioned.

"No, Mom, it's not true," I told her. I couldn't in my right mind tell her that I did. She would look at me differently. I wanted her approval, and I wouldn't get it if she saw me in a different light.

"You know he can't come back in our house?" she stated.

"And I don't blame you, Mom. But after what he did today, he and I are going our separate ways," I announced.

"Thank the Lord!" my mother rejoiced.

"Now you're using your head," my stepfather said, siding with me.

"I've got something else to say too," I added to get their undivided attention.

"What is it, baby?" my mother asked.

I tried to muster up the biggest smile I could make. "I've decided that I'm going to relocate to Miami, Florida, and practice law there."

"But you've just got back from Virginia!" she countered.

"Mom, I've been home for over a year. After I graduated and came back home, I spent most of my time here with you."

"She's right, honey." My stepfather sided with me.

"What about your bar exam? You're supposed to take it in a few days," she pointed out.

"I'm not going to take it. I'm going to find out when their next exam date is and then I'm going to fly down there and take it."

"But what's going to happen if you don't pass it? Stay there and take it again, or stay here in New York?" she probed.

"Mom, I will take it over and over, until I pass it. See, New York is my home, but I want to spread my wings. I want to experience life outside of the five boroughs. I want to open my bedroom curtains and see the ocean and the boats sailing by. I don't want all of the drama that's happening with me right now."

"So you're running away?" my stepfather interjected.

"No, but I desire to do this, so I've got to follow my heart."

"There's no way we can change your mind, huh?" my mother wanted to know.

"Nope. I've been thinking about making this move for a month or so now, and after Troy walked away from me today, it was confirmation that it was time for me to make that change."

My parents looked at each other, and then they looked back at me. My mother spoke first. "As bad as I don't want you to leave, I can't keep you here. It's your life, and whatever you do, I will support it."

"I agree with your mother," my stepfather added.

I smiled at them both. "I really appreciate you guys not giving me a hard time about it, because New York isn't doing it for me right now. Maybe later, if I feel differently, I'll come back. Who knows?"

"If you promise me that you won't go there, shack up with a guy, and get pregnant, then we have a deal," my mother said jokingly, but I knew that she was serious.

"Hey, I want grandkids," my stepfather said.

"I do too. But let her get married first," my mother commented.

He chuckled. "Well, yeah, I forgot about that part."

"So, have you thought about when you're going to make this transition?"

"After I find out when the exam date is in Florida, I'm going to put in my two weeks at the firm and then I'm going to leave. Being that Florida's laws are different from New

York's laws, I'm going to have to study all over again. So I want to be in Florida when I start doing it."

"Have you figured out where you're going to stay?" My mother's questions seemed endless. She was one nosey lady.

"I have a best friend that I met and used to hang out with while going to ODU. She lives in Miami, so she said that I could stay with her until I find my own place."

"Has she taken the bar?" my stepfather wondered aloud.

"Yes, she has, and she passed. She's currently working for law enforcement, but she plans to become a DEA agent."

"Wow! That's a kick-ass career choice," my stepfather commented.

"Yeah, it is, huh?"

"Well, I don't want you becoming an agent. I want you to become an attorney and ultimately become a senior partner. So don't get sidetracked," my mother reminded me.

"Mom, I know. I know," I assured her. "You guys have made me exhausted, and now I'm really going to go and take a long, hot bath. Wash off all of the drama I had today."

"You do that and I'm going to start cooking," she advised me.

"Okay. Love you guys."

I went back into my bedroom and lay down on my bed. I swear, a headache from all of this drama collapsed on top of me. My heart felt torn and my head was spinning in circles. It was hard for me to collect my thoughts. One minute, Troy was confessing his love for me, and then the next second, he's trying to attack me. And then to bring the drama to my parents' home had taken this thing to another level. I didn't know what to do.

While I lay there on my pillow, it dawned on me that I still had the bag of cocaine tucked away inside of my pillowcase. I sat up on my bed, reached into my pillowcase, grabbed the plastic bag, and pulled it out. There it was—a miniature Ziplock bag of cocaine in the center of the palm of my hand—and I couldn't believe it. I also couldn't believe how Martin had the balls to ask me if I saw it on the floor after he walked away from me the other day. He must have been high. Or this was some good stuff.

Curious about how potent this drug was, I opened it and smelled it first. It wasn't a strong smell, but I could smell a chemical, and it wasn't that bad. As my curiosity grew, I stuck my pinky finger down into the bag and pulled out a small mountain of the powder. It sat there like a pile of snow at the end of my fingernail, so I put my fingernail inside of my nostril and snorted it.

I swear, my vision went black, and when I opened my eyes, it looked like I saw stars. My nose started burning too, but then several seconds later, the drug shot up into my brain and it felt like my entire body was spinning around in circles. I wanted to get off my bed and start doing jumping jacks, and then I wanted to run up and down the hallway of my parents' apartment. A minute later, I felt dizzy, so I lay back on my bed and closed my eyes. And that's when things went to another level.

I saw everyone from ODU in my head. My best friend, Maria. Everyone. They were giggling and telling me how good the coke was and that they missed me. My roommate that committed suicide was there too. She was smiling at me and combing my hair with her fingers. She couldn't stop telling me how pretty I was and how she missed me. She even told me not to worry about her because she was with God and everything was good. She said that God was taking care of her. I was glad to hear her say all of that, because in a way, I felt somewhat responsible for her death. But now she said she was good, and that was all I needed to know.

Simon was there too. He was lavishing me with gifts galore. I had everything—a penthouse apartment, a Mercedes-Benz, huge diamonds, diamond necklaces, money—you name it, he gave it to me. He would also stop by and fuck me. He couldn't fuck at all. His dick was the smallest penis that I had ever seen. He laughed at me after he climbed off me. He said, "You thought I had a black man's dick, huh? Well, I fooled you, black girl. Now deal with it."

Simon lay in the bed next to me and laughed like he was a red-nosed clown. I couldn't figure out why he was laughing so hard. It was strange. And then Martin popped up, out of nowhere. "I fucking knew it. I knew you had my coke the whole time. But you tried to deny it. You're a liar. You know that. You're not a nice person. You're a sneaky little black girl. I'm going to tell Aaron and Noah that I'm not the only one in this firm."

Everyone would rear their face in a bubble, say a few things to me, and then the bubble would pop. I lay there as the drug took its effect on me. It felt like I was in another world and away from my reality. I was riding high on a cloud, and I didn't want to come down from it. It felt good. I never wanted this to end.

"Yoshi, are you eating dinner with your stepfather and me?" I heard my mother yell from the other side of my bedroom door.

Her voice startled me. I scrambled up and tried to sit upright in my bed, and when I did that, what was left of the coke spilled out onto the floor. "Just make me a plate and put it in the microwave," I instructed her as I struggled to get down on the floor and pick up the cocaine before she decided that she wanted to come into my bedroom.

"Okay. I can do that," she replied, and then I heard her walk away from my bedroom door. I was literally on the floor of my bedroom, trying to dust away the coke to prevent getting caught with it. And while doing it, I completely lost my high. I mean, it literally just evaporated into thin air. And what was so crazy about the whole thing was that I had no more to get high with later. All of the contents of the bag were empty. Gone. Kaput. Finished.

"Fuck, Mom, why the hell did you have to bother me at this particular time? You should've been reading a damn magazine or something. Shit!" I griped. I was getting angrier by the second, thinking about how she fucked up my air.

Now I see why drug addicts don't like sober people hanging around them. It's like oil and water. They're asking you why you're getting high, and saying that it isn't good for you, while you're trying to enjoy it. It's crazy.

10

Troy

I'm glad I walked away from Yoshi when I did. Because if I would've sat there and listened to more of her lies, I probably would've strangled her. Aaron was right not to get involved with that slut. I was a fool to believe the bullshit she was selling me. I mean, if Simon raped her, then why was she accepting flowers from him?

I guess the only way I'd find out was if I went to the source. I couldn't go to Simon, but I could call Aaron, and what better time to call than now, since I was stuck in this New York City traffic. He answered my call on the second ring.

"Yes, Troy. How can I help you, son?" Aaron greeted me.

"I just saw Yoshi and she says that Simon raped her," I boldly stated.

"She did what?" Aaron said. I could hear the shock in his voice.

"She's accusing Simon of raping her," I repeated.

"Those are some very serious accusations. And let me

guess, she says that it was done in my home?" Aaron commented.

"Yes. That's exactly where she said it happened."

"How dare she say Simon raped her?! Simon is a man of integrity. He would never do such a thing. She must be silenced at once." The sound of Aaron's voice indicated to me that he was very angry and turned off by these allegations. "Didn't I just tell you that she was bad news?" he added.

"Yes, you did," I replied reluctantly.

"Where did you see her?"

"At my apartment. She came to get her things," I lied. I couldn't let Aaron know that I went by her parents' apartment to confront her.

"Did she say anything about pressing charges against Simon?" Aaron wanted to know.

"I asked her that question and she said that she wasn't."

"Good. Now all we have to do is get rid of her," Aaron replied, sounding calculating.

"Fire her," I suggested. I wanted her out of that firm immediately. There was no way that I would be able to work with her under these circumstances. I mean, she fucked a new client of the firm. Every time I looked at her, I was going to think about Simon pounding his meat inside of her. It would be torture for me.

"If we fire her now, she could come back with a lawsuit. She could get us for wrongful termination and she could go after Simon as well. She could definitely start a shit show," Aaron explained.

"If you could guess what happened that night, what would you say?" I asked Aaron. He was a very wise man and he knew the tricks of the trade. And if anyone could sum up that night, he could, opposite of the line he kept using, saying that he retired to his room early.

"Simon is a very respectful businessman. He wouldn't

stoop that low to rape a partially-paid intern. Give him more credit than that. Yoshi is a grown woman and he is a grown man, so maybe they played around with one another. Innocent child's play between consensual adults. That's it. End of the story."

"Aaron, something about that situation still doesn't sit right with me."

"But it's gonna have to, son. This is not your fight. Leave well enough alone."

"So, how do we move on from here?"

"First things first, we have to monitor her. Make sure she doesn't change her mind and file a lawsuit against Simon. That would look pretty bad. I could see the fucking headlines in the *New York Times* now—*Builder and Developer Simon Howard Sued for Rape by One of Weinstein and Weinstein Law Firm's Employees*. First people are going to want to know where did this happen, and when they find out that the alleged incident happened at my residence, then they're going to ask where was I?" Aaron pointed out.

"Did you know that Simon sent her roses?"

"I think I did hear something about that."

"That doesn't bother you?"

"Why should it? Simon is a man; he can do what he wants."

"It doesn't wave a red flag that he's trying to silence her?"

"Troy, son, you're looking too deep into something that shouldn't concern you. Life looks bright for him on the other side of town. Leave him be."

"What if she files a lawsuit against him?" I asked. I was grasping for straws. "Did you not hear me this whole time when I said that she's insisting that he raped her?"

"Don't worry about her. I've got some things in place that would refute any claims that she may have. Trust me, I'm on top of it. Now, go on with your day. Go have an ice-cream cone or something," Aaron insisted. He was definitely booting me off his phone. I knew then that he was tired of me talking about Yoshi.

"Oh, before I forget, Noah and I pushed the date forward by a week for the annual party. There's a huge golf tournament in Florida and we will not miss it."

"Cool! Thanks for the heads-up."

"You're still coming, right?"

"Yes, sir."

"Bringing a guest?"

"As a matter of fact, I am."

"Great! Then we should celebrate and be merry," Aaron said. "You keep your head up, son. Everything will work out in the end," he added.

"And that I'm looking forward to."

11

Yoshi

Simon called my parents' house twice last night after I had the powwow with Troy, but both times my mother told him that I wasn't in. She questioned me about Simon's angle with pursuing me, especially after how angry Troy was when he left the house. I told her to mind her own business because my focus was on getting the hell out of New York and starting a new life in Miami, not about Simon and Troy.

I was surprised that I didn't hear from Troy last night after he left. Usually, when we argued, he'd let me calm down, or vice versa, and then we'd come back together within several hours or the next morning. It was 9:30 a.m. and he hadn't called. So I guess he really was over me. Well, good. Now I didn't have to worry about him trying to stop me from leaving New York.

When I arrived at work and stepped off the elevator, there was another vase filled with roses waiting for me. They were placed in the same spot on the receptionist desk, like the one from yesterday. She smiled at me and said, "Whoever is sending you these roses is truly smitten with you."

"It looks that way, huh?" I replied. I grabbed the vase filled with the flowers and carried them to my office. Thankfully, when I got there, Jillian wasn't anywhere in sight. She was such a fucking buzzkill and I didn't need her bad energy around me.

I set the vase down on my desk, clocked in on my computer, and then I grabbed the note placed in the center of the flowers. When I opened the card, it read: *You thought it was Simon, huh? Well, these roses aren't from Simon. They're from me, Troy, you piece-of-fucking-shit slut. You're going to regret fucking me over.*

Shocked by Troy's message, I immediately got up from my desk. I walked to the ladies' room, poured the water out of the vase, and then I placed the vase and the flowers in the trash can. "Fucking asshole," I hissed, and then I headed back to my desk.

En route, I ran into Noah. "Hi there, pretty lady. How are you?" he asked. He and I were the only ones in the hallway, until Jillian came walking around the corner.

"I'm great. And you?" I asked him.

"I'm doing great. Oh, and there goes another beauty," he announced. But Jillian was not a beauty. She was very basic.

"Thank you! And just the person I wanted to see," she said, looking directly at me. "Did you clock in yet?" she wondered aloud.

See, I saw right through that question. She wanted to insinuate to Noah that I might be late. So I told her I did and shut her mouth right up. "Yes, as a matter of fact, I did. You weren't sitting at your desk when I dropped my purse off and stuck it inside of my desk drawer."

"Okay, well, great, because I need you to draft a letter to one of our clients," she said, and handed me a manila folder.

I took it and said, "I'm on it." But what I really wanted to say: *Bitch, you are so phony! You were really trying to throw me underneath a bus.*

"Well, don't let me stop you ladies from keeping this ship running," Noah commented, and then he walked away.

"Go to your desk and start on it, and I'll be in there soon. I'm getting ready to have a meeting with Aaron."

"Okay."

I went one way, and Jillian and Noah went another way. It seemed like the farther in the opposite direction she walked, the better the atmosphere became. She was a devil in sheep's clothing and she was gunning for me. Fortunately for me, I wasn't going to be around much longer, being that I was relocating down south. So whatever intern they got to take my place would suffer all of the bullshit she was going to throw their way. Not me.

The moment I got back to my desk, I started drafting the letter. Halfway through it, I got a call. "Hi, Yoshi, I have a call for you on line four," Natalie announced on my speaker-phone.

"Did they say who they were?" I wanted to know. Because I had a strong suspicion that it was Troy.

"She identified herself as your mother."

"Okay, send her through," I instructed the receptionist.

I grabbed the receiver of my phone after the call came through. "Hey, Mom, what's up?" I asked her.

"Do you know that when your stepfather and I left to go out this morning, all four tires on our cars were slashed?" she said, and it was pretty clear that she was upset. Her voice sounded so alarming.

Hearing my mother upset like this had taken me aback. Anxiety crept into my entire body, making me feel very uneasy. "Where are you now?"

"I'm in the house. Your stepfather is outside waiting on AAA to get here and tow our cars to the tire dealership to get new tires."

"Mom, I am so sorry that happened to you guys. Have you called the police so they could come by and take a report?"

"Yes, we're waiting on them to come here as well."

"Were you guy's cars the only car tires that got slashed?"

"Yes, we were. So there is no question in my mind who was behind this."

"Who do you think did it?"

"Troy. He is the only one with motive. Remember, he didn't want to leave my house when I told him to?"

"Yes."

"Well, then, there you go."

"Is that what you're going to tell the cops?"

"As a matter of fact, I am," she said. "Hey, wait, someone is knocking at the front door. It might be the police now," she informed me.

"Well, check that out and I'll see you guys when I get home later."

"You be careful. He might try to slash your tires next."

"While I don't doubt that, let's just hope that it's kids running around playing pranks."

"That incident wasn't done at the hands of kids, and the security cameras outside will prove it."

"Okay, Mom, just take it easy and I'll see you later," I told her.

"All right, baby," she replied.

Immediately after I hung up with my mother, I called Troy's home phone. I knew that I was forbidden to call him again, and especially from this office, but he had barked up the wrong tree. First he tried to choke the daylights out of me after catching me carrying a vase full of roses given to me by Simon. Then he confronted me in front of my parents, threatening not to leave their home, cursed me out and called me all kinds of *slut* and *whore* names, and then he sent me flowers this morning with an attached note that called me more insults. But what was really fucked up was that he had vandalized my parents' cars. Now to do messed-up stuff to me was tolerable, but then to fuck with my parents was a no-no. And I was going to let him know how I felt about it.

"Hello," he said.

"You have a fucking nerve to send me flowers with a distasteful note in it. But then to turn around and harass my parents is going below the belt. And it's foul too."

He chuckled. "So you got my flowers, huh?"

"Fuck you, Troy! You're a miserable-ass man and I will not tolerate your bullshit!"

"Tell me, what you're going to do about it?"

"For starters, the cops are at my parents' house and they are filing a vandalism report against your ass. You just can't go around slashing people's tires because you're upset with me and you can't get your way."

"I didn't vandalize your parents' tires. And this security camera you're talking about will prove that," he said snidely.

"We all know that you're a smart man. So tell me, who did you pay to do it?"

"I have no earthly idea what you're talking about. Trust me, I have better things to do with my money and my time."

"Bullshit! Then tell me, why the note with the roses? You're that brokenhearted that you've got to stoop so low? You're upset that Simon fucked me better than you?" I spoke, gnashing my teeth together. Even though I didn't remember Simon having sex with me the other night, I felt like if I switched my story and said otherwise, then it would hurt Troy's heart. Men don't like hearing about other men's sexual performances, especially if they take the backseat to the other man. See, Troy brought this tongue-lashing on himself. He didn't have to send me that card with the roses and have someone damage my parents' cars. He could've left well enough alone and we would not be having this conversation.

"You dirty whore! Do you know that I could have you fired with the snap of my finger?" he roared through the phone, and I knew then that I had ruffled his feathers. I actually got a kick out of it, considering what he had done to my parents' cars. But let's not forget the incident when he put his hands on me.

"Oh, so now I'm dirty?"

"You've always been dirty. I only used you up and spit you out."

"And here I thought that you were a nice guy. Very respectful! Generous and kindhearted. But, boy, did you fool me," I commented.

"And I thought that you were a wholesome girl. Turns out you're damaged goods. A piece of trash. I swear, I should've listened to the partners of the firm."

"You should've, because we wouldn't be having this talk. But guess what? I'm out of here. I'm moving to Florida and I am not looking back. You, and whoever else, can take this position and shove it right up your ass! Because there's better things waiting for me down south."

"Oh, so you're leaving, huh?"

"You damn right I'm leaving."

"And when is this happening?"

"None of your damn business. I've told you enough, now get lost," I said, and then I disconnected his ass.

How dare that asshole say all of that to me? He had changed so drastically. I'd never ever pictured Troy talking to and treating me this way. Just a few days ago, we discussed that the senior partners might have his entire apartment and telephones bugged. Fast-forward to today, he was singing a different tune. Was he diagnosed with a bipolar disorder and I didn't know about it? Damn! What did I get myself mixed up in?

Today definitely seemed like another long day. Jillian micromanaged me, wanting to know if I was done with the drafted letter. Then I had to fill out all of the spreadsheets for the attorney's clients. After that, she wanted to know if I followed up with the client thank-you letters. I mean, it was one thing after the other. For some reason, today seemed more stressed than the other days. Had someone pulled her coat about what Troy and I were going through? Or was she giving me a harder time because she wanted me to just up and quit? I couldn't say right now what was up her sleeve, but whatever it was, I was going to make it really easy for her and leave when I was ready. And the way things were going, I might not give them two weeks' notice. Yeah . . . that's exactly what I was going to do.

On my way to my car, I watched over my shoulders with every step I took. I didn't want Troy sneaking up on me and surprising me with his pop-up confrontations. And, thankfully, the coast was clear. I got to my car and out of the parking garage with no hiccups. I even arrived at my parents' home with no problems. They weren't there, so I assumed that they were out handling their affairs with their cars.

Tired from today's hectic day, I disrobed, got into the shower, and once I was done with that, I slipped into a pair of sweatpants and T-shirt. I went into the TV room and powered on the television. After sifting through the channels, I settled for watching *Family Feud*. During the bonus round, the telephone rang.

I answered it on the second ring. "Hello," I answered.

"Hi there, gorgeous," the gentleman replied. I knew then it was Simon's voice right after he said the word *hi*.

"Hi," I greeted him back. But in all honesty, I wasn't in the mood to talk to him, especially after the powwow I had with Troy earlier. I was mentally drained, so I knew that I wasn't going to be on the phone with him for long.

"How was your day?"

"It was long, but I got through it," I told him. As badly as I wanted to tell him what my day really was like, I knew that it wouldn't be appropriate. But then after thinking about it, having sex with me while I was drunk wasn't appropriate either.

"Have you had dinner yet?"

"Yes, I just ate," I lied, because I knew the next comment would be *Let's go to dinner.*

"What a shame. I had something planned for you."

"Can I get a rain check?"

"Why, most certainly. What about tomorrow?"

"What time?"

"How does eight o'clock sound?"

"Eight o'clock sounds good."

"Perfect. Well, I'm going to let you get back to what you were doing, and I'll see you tomorrow."

"Awesome," I said with as much enthusiasm that I could muster up.

I couldn't wait to get off the telephone with Simon. I was so confused about everything going on around me. I had to deal with Troy and his mental abuse, Jillian's micromanaging ass, Aaron and his manipulating ass, and now Simon. I swear, the quicker I got out of New York, the better I would be, because the longer I was here, the more fucked up in the head I became.

12

Troy

"Hey, Tee, what will it be?" Brad, the bartender, asked me.

"My usual," I told him after I sat down on a stool at the bar. "It's pretty slow tonight, huh?" I added after I looked around.

"Yeah, for now. My Tuesday-night crowd starts trickling in here around eight, eight thirty," he informed me, and then he placed a shot of whiskey down on the bar directly in front of me. I picked it up and poured every drop of it into my mouth.

"Oggghhh," I said, trying to contain the heat it brought to my throat and swallow it at the same time.

"Pour me another one," I instructed him. So he poured another shot of whiskey into my shot glass and I put it to my mouth and devoured every ounce of it. "Oggghhh," I said, simultaneously clearing my throat and raising up the shot glass in my hand for Brad to pour me another round. He filled my shot glass up again, but instead of me drinking it, I set it down on the bar in front of me so I could take in the effects the first two drinks had given me.

"Slow down, mate. It isn't Coca-Cola," he advised me.

I looked up at Brad and cracked a smile. "Now you tell me," I commented.

"What's on your mind?"

Before I answered him, I picked up my last shot of whiskey, put it to my lips, and poured every drop into my mouth. "Oggghhh," I said, clearing my throat as the alcohol traveled down it. After I set the glass down, I looked up at Brad and said, "Having women problems."

"Mate, that's one of the reasons men come in here to drink," he replied nonchalantly. "Are you talking about the same woman?" he added.

"Yeah, that's the bitch! Just found out that she slept with one of the firm's clients."

"Ahhh, that's a bad one," Brad commented as he used a hand towel to wipe away small glass rings of water from the bar.

"Tell me about it."

"Does she know that you know?"

"Yes, of course. When I found out, I questioned her about it and the bitch lied to me. But I pressured her to tell me the truth and she finally did."

"Was she remorseful about it?"

"At first, she was. But as the conversation went on, she threw it in my face, like she was given a badge of honor of some sorts."

"What did you do?"

"I choked her with my bare hands. I swear, if I had a fucking gun, I probably would've shot and killed her."

"Well, I'm glad that you didn't have one on hand. Mate,

you'd be in prison right now waiting to go to trial for murder, and I'm sure you wouldn't want that."

I looked in the mirror behind the bar. "What's wrong with me? I'm a good-looking guy, right?"

"Yeah, you're a good-looking guy. And that's why you can leave here right now and pick up any woman you want."

"But I want her," I said after turning my attention back toward Brad.

"Isn't this girl you're talking about black? I remember the last time you spoke of her, you said that she was a black woman."

"Yeah, she's black, and I remind her of it all of the time. When she finally fessed up to sleeping with the firm's client, I called her *black bitch*, *black whore*—you name it, I said it."

"Wow! That's heavy. But it sounds like you're happy that you said it."

"I am. What would you do if you found out your girlfriend cheated on you? And it wasn't a regular guy, he's a fucking rich guy."

"How did she explain it happening?" Brad's questions continued.

"She said she was under the influence and he took advantage of her."

"Do you believe it?"

"I can't say I did. But after I kept pressuring her to tell me the truth, she said that she had sex with him willingly and that it was fucking great. Brad, I swear to you, man, I would've killed her on the spot if I had a gun," I reiterated.

"Like I said before, I am really glad that you didn't."

"Brad, a woman is never supposed to tell another man that the guy she's sleeping with now is better than the last guy. I mean, there's lines that you just don't cross. How can you come back from that?"

"Yeah, that's a hard pill to swallow," he agreed, and then he said, "Mate, what are you going to do now?"

"I don't know. Part of me wants to kill her with my bare hands, but then something washes over me and I want her back. You know she mentioned to me that she's relocating to Miami," I shared.

"Did she tell you when?"

"No, but from what I gathered from our conversation, she's leaving soon."

"So, what are you going to do? Talk her out of it or what?"

"I want to, but then I feel like every time I look at her, I'm going to think about her fucking the rich guy."

"Have you thought about having a conversation with the rich guy?"

"The senior partners at the firm wouldn't allow it. They'd fire me on the spot if I confronted him. And get this, the guy sent her yellow roses. And ask me what I did?"

"What did you do?"

"I fucking smashed them up. Completely destroying the vase that they came in."

"Did you ask her why he sent her roses?"

"She downplayed it. But come on, Brad, the guy either thanked her for fucking him or he wants to continue pursuing her. You know, maybe take her on a date or something."

"Sounds like you have a lot to think about."

"What would you do in a situation like this?" I asked Brad. I seriously needed some advice. I couldn't go to Noah or Aaron and ask for their advice. They'd both laugh me right out of their office.

"Call the exotic dancer that you met in here a few nights ago. As a matter of fact, she came in here, day before yesterday, and asked about you. She wanted to know two things—

when was the last time I saw you, and why hadn't you returned her phone calls?"

"Brad, you know me. I've gotta clear up one thing before I can get into another."

"All she wants is for you to tame her and give her some good loving. I'm sure you're gonna have to spend some money on her too. She looks expensive."

"Come on, Brad, forget her. I want some words of wisdom for the young girl I'm hooked up with now."

"Mate, that's a hard one right there. See, I've never dated a black woman before."

"What would you do if she was a white woman?"

Brad smiled. "I can't answer that, because I can't get it out of my head that she's black."

"All right, fuck it. Pour me another shot," I instructed him.

It was clear that Brad wanted no part of my conversation, so I left well enough alone and got him to pour me two more shots. By the time I left the bar, I had drunk a total of seven shots of whiskey. I can't tell you how I got home, especially since I was so inebriated.

When I woke up the following morning, I got hit with the hardest hangover ever. My head was spinning around in circles. The ripples in my stomach were rumbling, and nausea immediately reared its ugly head. I lay there, trying to figure out if I should go out today. Normally, when I get hangovers, they aren't this severe. I guess I needed to suck it up, take a couple of Bayer aspirins, and be back in shape in no time.

As I had figured, my headache did subside and I felt like a new man. What hadn't gone away was the burning desire to see Yoshi. The love-hate relationship that had grown inside of me would not let me get her out of my mind. The burning sensation of hurting her physically, and then consoling her immediately thereafter, had become a fixture in my heart. What was I going to do?

After mulling over ways to get over it, I couldn't come up with any solutions. I did, however, decide to go back to work. The black eye, which my client's bodyguard gave me, had healed. There was a small spot of discoloration underneath my eyelid, but it wasn't that significant where you could see it four to five feet away. Within arm's distance of me, yes. Other than that, no. And to have no appointments today gave me more reason to go to work. The only people I would see would be the other partners and staff, and I was cool with that. My only challenge would be working around Yoshi. But since I wanted to see her, I got dressed and headed to work.

Natalie, the receptionist, greeted me after I exited the elevator. I greeted her back without looking in her direction. She knew that I was still upset with her for calling Aaron to save Yoshi. Whether she knew it or not, I've got clout in this firm, and the next time she called one of the senior partners on me, she was out of here for good. After doing my best to avoid locking eyes with the receptionist, I saw a bouquet of yellow roses through my peripheral vision. This sight sent me into a fit of rage. I stopped in my tracks, turned my direction toward the receptionist's desk, and then I grabbed the vase filled with the yellow roses. I headed in the direction of the men's restroom. As soon as I entered it, I dropped the vase into the garbage can.

Feeling no ways about it, I exited the restroom and walked directly to my office. Once inside, I took a seat behind my desk and started checking my emails. I had a total of over two hundred. Only a third of them were important and needed responses. While I began to work on the emails and returned them to the senders, Noah poked his head in my office and asked me to follow him.

"Can you give me a few minutes? I need to finish this email," I told him.

"Sure, come when you're done," he replied.

After Noah stepped away from my office door, a cloud of anxiety washed over my entire body, wondering why Noah wanted me to come to his office. I figured whatever he wanted, he should've addressed here in my office. Was it about the roses I disposed of? Had the receptionist ratted me out again? What could it be?

The second after I sent off the email, I stood up from my desk and braced myself to hear what Noah had to say. All sorts of things started running through my mind. I mean, he could want to talk to me about anything. We had a lot of interactions that built this foundation, so, hopefully, it concerned one of those.

With a rapid heartbeat, I headed to Noah's office. It was only twenty-five feet away, so getting there took less than thirty seconds, if that. When I turned the corner, I heard laughter. There were three voices. I immediately recognized the first two; they belonged to Noah and Aaron. The third voice came from a woman, but I couldn't figure out who it was, so I moved forward and entered Noah's office. Everyone's eyes lit up as soon as I appeared. And I zoomed in on the woman whose voice I hadn't recognized. Surprisingly, it came from Yoshi. It instantly became obvious that she had a case of laryngitis. She was sitting in a chair next to Aaron, while Noah sat behind his desk.

"Come on in and have a seat," Noah instructed me.

Consumed with a giant ball of trepidation, I walked

slowly to the available chair positioned near Noah. After I sat down, I glanced over at Yoshi, who was dressed in a dark blue two-piece suit. The length of her skirt came to her knees and it exposed her perfect, sleek legs. The stockings she wore were a nude color and they matched her skin color effortlessly. I hoped that she would give me eye contact, but she wouldn't. I only got her to look at me when I entered Noah's office. After that, she turned her attention toward Noah.

"How is everyone doing?" I started off the conversation. I spoke first because I was feeling a little awkward.

"Good. Good," Aaron chimed in.

I took a deep breath and exhaled after I sat down. "So, what's up?"

"Well, as we all know, you and Yoshi had an intimate relationship, up until just recently, when we told you and her both that it needed to stop," Noah started off saying.

"Yes, and we stopped it," I interjected.

"Yes, yes, we know," Aaron agreed.

"Well, since then, it has been brought to our attention that Yoshi's parents' vehicles had been vandalized," Noah stated.

"So that is what this is about?" I asked. I instantly felt like I was sideswiped.

"Hold up. Calm down, son. We are not placing the blame on you. We just wanted to bring this matter to your attention, that's all," Noah declared.

"So, if you're not blaming me, then why I am sitting here?" I wanted to know.

"Because you did it," Yoshi said, coming out of nowhere. Her crackly voice instantly irritated me.

"I didn't do shit!" I roared, and shot up on my feet.

"Well, if you didn't do it, then you had someone do it for

you," Yoshi accused. "And while you're at it, tell them why you threw the roses, which were delivered to me today, into the trash in the men's restroom!"

"Have a seat, Troy. Let's not make this issue bigger than it is," Aaron insisted.

"Yes, Troy, calm yourself down. You're not in a boxing arena," Noah added.

I sat back down in my seat and continued to defend myself. "Listen, you guys, I don't know what Yoshi has told you, but I had nothing to do with vandalizing her parents' vehicles. That's not even my character. I don't operate like that."

"So, who did you have do it?" Yoshi blurted out. It seemed like the more and more she talked, the less she could say her words clearly.

"I refuse to dignify that question with a response," I hissed at her, and turned my attention to Noah.

"That's because you're guilty." Yoshi was pressing the issue. She wouldn't let up. She knew that I had something to do with her parents' cars, but she didn't have the evidence.

"All right, all right, that's enough!" Noah shouted. Yoshi, Aaron, and I sat back and waited for Noah to finish his thought. "Troy, Aaron and I want the back-and-forth with you and Yoshi to stop. She will only take orders from Jillian, Aaron, and me. That way, you two wouldn't have any reason to communicate."

"Is that it? Because that is easy," I said gladly. As much as I wanted to see her when I came into work today, having her sitting in Noah's office, ratting me out, I wanted to be done with her, once and for all. There was no going back for me.

"What about the roses? Can we address that?" Yoshi added.

"Yes, Troy, let's do that. What made you do it?" Noah questioned me.

"I'll tell you what, let's address the sudden case of laryngitis. Did you get it from sucking on Simon's genitals?!" I roared. I swear, I couldn't hold back. She had pushed my last button.

"Come on, Troy, that wasn't necessary. Apologize to Yoshi," Aaron interjected.

"Yes, that was way off," Noah added.

"No, he can keep his apologies. Let's talk about that black eye and why you got beat up. Tell your bosses how you're making promises to clients that you can't keep. They really socked it to him. His face was messed up pretty bad," she teased me.

"Try becoming an attorney first and then we can have this conversation. Remember that you're *just* an assistant," I blasted her.

"Troy, you can't be making promises to clients," Noah reminded me.

"Yes, Troy, we taught you that when you first started working here at the firm," Aaron said, agreeing with Noah.

"And that's not all. Troy, tell them that you think they're bugging your home phone line and car phone. Tell them how paranoid you were when you first suspected that they did it. Tell them how you talked shit about them, Troy," she blurted out.

I can't believe that this fucking girl just exposed me in front of my two bosses. What she didn't know was that I had already addressed the tapping-and-bugging situation with Aaron. But let's say that I hadn't. I would be looking like a fool right now, so betrayal instantly engulfed me. I was staring straight at her, but I didn't see her. I saw a conniving-ass bitch, and I wanted to choke the breath out of her. I mean, how dare she insinuate to Noah and Aaron that I didn't trust them? That I talked about them? Did she realize how this looked?

"Cat gotcha tongue?" she taunted me.

"Don't listen to this bitch, you guys. She's fucking delusional," I pointed out while grinding my teeth together. If I knew for sure that I wouldn't go to jail today, I would smash her face right now.

"Troy, just calm down a moment before this gets out of hand," Aaron interceded.

"Yes, I've heard enough from the both of you," Noah agreed.

"It has already gotten out of hand," I pointed out. "But since we're on a roll here, tell both Noah and Aaron that Simon raped you inside of Aaron's home, after Aaron left you two alone," I added.

I was fucking burning up on the inside. And even though I had already addressed the situation about Simon, I wanted to see the sheer humiliation on her face. In her mind, this would be the first time both Noah and Aaron found out about her allegations. My confession to them would make her look really bad. But more important, they'd see her as a whistleblower. Who trusts someone after finding out that they're talking behind your back? Not too many people I know.

Aaron and Noah looked at me, and then they turned their attention toward Yoshi. "Yoshi, is that what you think?" Aaron asked her. I swear, he could get an Oscar for the way he was acting, and Noah sat there in disbelief.

"That's not quite what I said," she started off. She was falling into my trap.

"Well, if I recall, you said that after Aaron left you and Simon in the cigar lounge of his penthouse, you and Simon had a few more drinks, and then everything around you went black. The following morning, you woke up in one of the guest rooms naked, and when you felt yourself, you were soaking wet. You told me that you knew that Simon raped you, because you knew that you didn't give him permission to fuck you. Now am I lying or what?" I snapped. I was burying her deeper and deeper into the grave she had dug out for me.

Aaron abruptly stood up from his chair. "Troy, now that is enough. We are not running a circus here!" he roared.

"I swear, if I'd known that you were this cutthroat and petty, I would not have given you the time of day," she managed to say.

"Yoshi, I want you to let it go!" Aaron shouted.

"Can I leave?" she asked Aaron after turning her attention toward him.

"Of course, you can leave. You hold no value here. These men here only hired you because they know your parents. That's it. You're not that fucking smart, like you think you are."

"Okay, enough, you two. Yoshi, go back to your desk. We'll handle things from here," Noah said.

"Good riddance," I blurted out as Yoshi stormed out.

After Yoshi left Noah's office, Aaron started pacing the floor from one side of the room to the next. "Do you see why we stress company policy of *not* getting romantically involved with colleagues? *Especially* with a fucking intern!" Aaron roared.

"Yes, Troy, you did a doozy with this one. I wonder who else she mentioned these rape allegations to," Noah chimed in.

"I haven't the foggiest idea," Aaron said.

"Aaron, you know her stepfather very well. Is she close to her parents?" Noah wondered aloud.

"Don't worry, she hasn't had that conversation with them," I assured them both.

"What about a favorite cousin or best friend? Does she have any of them?" Noah's questions continued.

"As far as I know, all of her friends are back in college," I informed them.

"Just how long have you been banging that young girl?" Noah asked me.

"Since she first started working here," Aaron said, and then he sat back down in his chair.

"You don't waste any time, do you?" Noah commented.

Aaron chuckled. "His mother and father would turn over in their graves if they knew that he was banging a young black girl."

"Tell me about it," I said, and chuckled. Because Aaron was right, my family would not have approved of me seeing a black girl. This was the way I was raised. But a small part of me didn't want to be that way.

"Have you taken her around your friends or gambling buddies?" Aaron added.

"No," I answered him.

"Noah, do you remember when I told you that he denied even spending time with her, when I first brought it to his attention?"

"Of course, I do. We knew what was going on between you two before Aaron confronted you about it," Noah pointed out to me. "Honestly, do you have feelings for that girl?"

"I liked her, if that's what you want me to say. But I hate her fucking guts now," I confessed. But it was a lie. I was still in love with Yoshi. That's why I'd been going through these fits of rage.

"Troy, you destroyed her bouquet of roses, so, of course, there's feelings there. Who do you think you're kidding?" Aaron stated.

"Do you know who sent them?" Noah asked me.

"Yes, I do. Aaron does too. And it's obvious that he's pursuing her," I didn't hesitate to say.

"None of this shit would be happening now if you would've kept your dick in your pants!" Aaron blurted out. He was really aggravated by my actions.

"Do you think that she may be a problem?" Noah looked at Aaron and me.

"At this point, I don't know," I replied first.

"She said a lot of shit in here just now, so in my opinion, she's a loose cannon," Aaron answered.

"I think we should let Simon know what's going on. That way, he won't be blindsided with a lawsuit," I suggested.

Noah and Aaron laughed at me.

"Are you fucking insane? Do you know how much money we'd lose if we opened our mouths?" Aaron disagreed.

"I take it, he doesn't know?" Noah asked Aaron.

"Doesn't know what?" I asked them both. I was confused.

"The whole thing with Yoshi and Simon was staged," Aaron said.

"*Staged*? Staged how?" I pressed the issue.

"I made all of the cocktails that night at my place. I spiked Yoshi's drink first. I spiked Simon's drink right before I left them in the cigar lounge alone. Yoshi gave him a massage and grew restless, so Simon took her to the bedroom and laid her down on the bed. She pushed him away a few times, but her strength was no match for his. He undressed her and started fondling her, and before he could finish, he fell asleep in the bed, between her legs. Tim, the firm's investigator, came in, undressed Simon, put him in some compromising positions, and took a dozen photos of them. We even took some photos of him wearing black bondage clothing, and some of him wearing our Klansman white hoods. The photos were timeless," Aaron added, and then he chuckled.

"Why do that?" I wanted to know more.

"It's called blackmail, son. See, Simon is worth a lot of money. We could generate millions of dollars each year from his company, with a clause we put in his contract that would give us thirty percent of his gross, and it cannot be changed even in a bad economy. Now if he tries to block us from doing that, we threaten to release those photos of him sleeping with a black girl in spiked leather bondage clothing. If the association of sleeping with a black girl doesn't ruin him, then wearing a white KKK hood will, considering he has investors and board members that are of African-American and Hispanic descent."

"Is that legal?" I asked them both, even though I already knew the answer.

"Of course not." Noah chuckled again.

"So Yoshi really *didn't* have sex with Simon?"

"Nope. We're geniuses, right?" Aaron boasted.

"I take it that this isn't the first time you guys did this?" I wondered.

"Of course not, how do you think we've amassed the wealth we have?" Aaron continued.

I swear, looking at these two motherfuckers tell me that this whole thing with Yoshi and Simon was staged had my mind boggled. I was actually fucking livid, because this whole time, I thought that Yoshi fucked that guy, but she didn't. She was the victim in all of this, not the perpetrator. How could I make this right? How could I go back and tell her that I was sorry?

"She's leaving and relocating to Florida because of this," I mentioned.

"That's great news. But let's keep in mind that one day she

could wake up and decide that she wants to file charges. And because she was in your home, she could involve you too," Noah pointed out to Aaron.

"Well, she's got to go," Aaron said.

"How?" Noah wanted Aaron to explain.

"At our annual party," Aaron replied.

Noah thought for a second. "I think you're onto something. But who would take her on?" Noah wanted to know.

"I'll do it," Aaron said.

"Awesome," Noah volunteered.

"No, I'll do it," I blurted out. In my heart, I couldn't have either one of these guys put their grimy hands on Yoshi.

"Are you still seeing your doctor?" Noah continued to question.

"Of course, I am. Why?" I asked.

"Because you've been flip-flopping a lot lately," Noah declared.

"I agree. I first saw it when he lied to me about seeing Yoshi. And then this recent incident with the flowers," Aaron explained.

"Are you taking your meds?" Noah pressed the issue.

"Yes, I am," I admitted.

"Have you missed a day?" Aaron asked.

"A few times. But I doubled up if I forgot to take the one from the day before," I assured them.

"If we let you join in on the games, you can't screw this up, Troy," Aaron insisted.

"Yes, Troy, Aaron is right. You cannot fumble the ball. If you do, then we would be forced to deal with what's best for our firm. Now, are you sure about this?" Noah asked.

"Before I answer that, will Simon be attending this year's annual party?" I asked both men.

"Yes, he has been invited. But he wishes not to bring a guest," Aaron spoke up.

"Does he know about the game we play once a year?" I wanted to know.

"In so many words, yes."

I thought for a second and then I said, "Okay, well, I will do it."

Noah and Aaron looked at one another and smiled, and then they looked back at me. "Well, then, it's settled," Noah stated.

13

Yoshi

Those motherfuckers thought I walked away from the door to Noah's office, but I stood there and heard everything. To hear Noah ask Troy if he thought I would be a problem was frightening. What was going to happen if they thought that I would be a problem? And then to hear that Simon and I never had sex nearly knocked me out. On the one hand, I was excited and relieved at the same time. Here I was thinking that Simon raped me, but he hadn't. He even thought that we had sex, but he passed out before he could do anything. To know that this was staged was beyond comprehensible.

These guys were so scandalous. I wondered what would Simon do if he found out that there were photos of us dressed in sexual bondage attire, and with him wearing a white KKK hood? I swear, I wanted to tell him so bad, but I couldn't trust that he wouldn't rat me out. So, I guess, the best thing I could do was play my position until I was out of this place.

I could hear the change in Troy's voice after he realized that I hadn't had sex with Simon. His demeanor did a one-eighty. He seemed calm while he asked both Noah and Aaron a bunch of questions about the setup between Simon and me. To think that this fucker did this was insane! Until now, I had a lot of respect for those guys in that office. I didn't ask for this shit. I didn't ask to attend that dinner meeting at Aaron's penthouse. I came to this firm to learn from a group of respected and highly sought-after attorneys in the state of New York, and this is the shit I get?!

Now to hear that Troy had a fucking shrink took me for a loop. I fucking knew it. I knew something was wrong with his unstable ass. He really was bipolar. And he took meds for it. Now I knew why he went from one extreme to the other. One minute he was in love with me, and then the next, he was ready to put his hands on me. If anyone should be sued, it was him. I swear, he had one more time to put his hands on me and it was going to be war.

From all of the things said about me during the conversation between Troy and the senior bosses, what hurt me the worst was to hear them tell Troy that his parents would be turning over in their graves if they knew he was seeing a black woman. That was the most racist shit ever! I mean, I knew that after Troy hurled a lot of racist slurs at me in our most recent arguments that he must've been raised by racist parents, but I didn't know that it was this severe.

Damn, I wished that I had known it sooner, because I would not have ever entered him on no level. Who would've thought that racism would still plague this world, and especially in New York? Black people escaped the South and relocated here and in states farther up north. The states in the North were deemed safe havens, so who would've known that racism was still around?

After Troy and the senior bosses talked about me like I

was black trash, I figured I had heard enough and snuck away from the office door. When I got back to my seat, Jillian wasn't sitting at her desk, and I was relieved about that. She eventually came back to her desk a couple of hours later. I found out that she had to make a run to the courts to file documents for one of Aaron's clients. Her absence felt good while it lasted.

Troy tried a couple of times to get me to talk to him, but I wouldn't let him get close to me. From there, I avoided contact with him for the rest of the day. I almost quit and walked out of the firm, at least a dozen times. To know that I was alone in this place made me feel helpless. Going to Florida looked like the winning idea. The only thing was, I had to wait to get my affairs in order before I left. I guess now was the time to start getting my ducks in a row.

When I got home, I was told by my mother that Simon had called and I should return his call. Because of everything that happened to me earlier, I dreaded calling him. I really wasn't in the mood to talk. I just wanted to take a long, hot shower and go to bed.

"Hello, beautiful!" he greeted me after answering my call on the second ring.

"Hi, Simon," I replied with little enthusiasm.

"Are you ready for tonight?" he asked.

"Oh my God, Simon. I am sorry. I truly forgot about tonight. See, I had a rough day at work and I am not in a mental state to entertain," I stated.

"I'm sorry to hear that. But you promised. So you got to stick to your promise," he reminded me, and then chuckled.

But I found nothing to laugh about. As badly as I wanted to tell him to leave me alone, it quickly dawned on me that Simon could be an asset to me . . .

"Where would you like to take me for dinner?" I changed my tune.

"Wow! Telling you that I wasn't taking no for an answer was all I had to do, huh?"

"I love a take-charge kind of guy."

"Well, guess what?"

"What?"

"Then I'm your type of guy," he assured me. "Can you be ready within the hour?"

"Yes."

"Great, I will have one of my drivers pick you up and take you to this nice and quaint place on the Upper East Side, so put on something beautiful and I'll see you then."

"Sounds like a plan."

"Then it's a plan indeed. And I'll see you shortly."

"Can't wait," I told him, and then we ended the call.

"And where are you going?" my mother asked me after she stepped into my bedroom. She looked at me from head to toe, admiring a black strapless cocktail dress she had bought me a year ago for the firm's annual charity event. That was the first time I met the senior partners.

Troy was at that event and I was introduced to him. He seemed nice. Very accommodating. He was funny too. He was known for telling very funny jokes. The young lady he was with didn't think so. She walked around like she had a stick up her ass. Troy ignored her for a large part of the night. He made it seem like she was the party pooper. Now that I think about it, he probably was treating her badly before they arrived at the party. Troy was definitely a class act.

"Simon is sending a car to pick me up," I told her while I was doing my makeup in front of the mirror.

"I don't think that's a good idea."

"Why? Because Troy said that I had sex with him?"

"I wasn't going to say that, but yes. Besides that, I don't think he's good for you."

"Mom, no one would ever be *good for me* in your eyes."

"Yeah, I suppose you're right. But this guy, I really have my doubts about."

"Why?"

"I think he has an agenda."

"What kind of agenda?"

"I can't quite put my finger on it."

"Mom, don't worry about me. I'm a big girl. I can handle myself."

"I think the jury is still out on that one."

"Look, he's just a friend. That's it."

"Why don't you find someone your own age?"

"You're acting like I'm getting into a new relationship."

"Lord God, I hope not."

"Mom, we're just going out to dinner. We're gonna talk about my future goals, places I want to go, among other things."

"Are you using this guy to get over Troy?"

"No, not at all."

"Good, because rebound relationships can get very complicated."

"Trust me, I'm ten steps ahead of you."

"Can I ask you a personal question?"

I let out a long sigh because I never knew where my mother was going to take a conversation. "Yes, you can."

"Are you afraid of Troy?"

"No, Mom, I am not afraid of Troy," I told her. And in reality, I was not. When I was alone with him, I was not able to read him, and that was not good for me. But, of course, I could not tell my mother that.

"Are you being forthcoming with me?"

"Yes, Mom, I am," I tried to assure her.

She held her stare on me for three to four seconds, like she was trying to see through me. I knew what that meant. She was waiting for me to fess up. But I was going to stand my ground. I couldn't have her worrying about me and my safety when it came to Troy. She couldn't handle that type of stress.

"Mom, what are you looking at?" I asked her. I needed to break her trance.

"I'm looking at you, hoping that you aren't lying to me. You know I worry a lot for you, especially after you lost your roommate to that drug overdose. Do you think about her?"

"Sometimes."

"Do you find yourself missing her?"

"Of course, Mom. We were roommates. We lived together."

"Have you reached out to her family?"

"No, but my other roommate does. She keeps me in the loop about things."

"You don't use drugs, right?"

"No, Mom, I don't," I answered her. But I got a little defensive about it, so I hoped that I didn't send up a red flag.

"If you were, would you tell me?" she pressed.

"Mom, you're acting really weird right now."

"I'm sorry, Yoshi. I just want you to be happy and do great things in this world. Is that too much for me to ask for?" She expressed her concern to me; I could tell that she was getting a little emotional.

"No, Mom, it isn't. But you've gotta stop worrying so much. I'm here with you. I'm alive. I'm healthy. What more can we ask for?"

"I guess you're right," she agreed. "But I'm your mother and you need to know that I'm gonna always be overbearing and concerned about your well-being," she added.

"And I have no problems with that. But keep it to a minimal," I said, and cracked a smile. I did it to lighten the mood.

My mother can get heavily sentimental at times. Who knows, maybe I will get that way when I have kids?

"So, did that gentleman say where you two were going?"

"No."

"Are you guys going out alone?"

I chuckled. "Yes, Mommy."

"Why are you laughing?"

"Because you're acting like I'm going out on a Sweet Sixteen birthday date."

"I know. I just want you to be safe. So I'm gonna let you use my Mace, just in case."

"For Simon?"

"Yes."

"Mom, he's a client to Mr. A. What could he do to me?"

"What if Troy sees you two together and tries to hurt you guys? The Mace would really come in handy then."

"Troy isn't that crazy. He knows that Simon is a big client to the Weinsteins, and if he jeopardized that, they would fire him on the spot. Simon is, like, a big deal around the firm. They've been trying to secure that deal with him for a long time."

"What if he comes here harassing you or us again?"

"Call the cops and then we'll file for a restraining order."

"And what if that doesn't work? Or what if he leaves before the cops get here? I see it on the news and read about psychopaths in the newspapers all of the time. They won't stop at anything until they kidnap or kill a person that they can't see another person have. It becomes an obsession for them. And I don't want a police detective knocking on my door bearing bad news about that guy doing something horrible to you. I swear, I would die inside."

"Mom, stop overreacting. Nothing like that will ever happen to us."

"I hope you're right."

"Speaking of which, this morning, Noah, Aaron, Troy, and I had a meeting. I brought up the issue about you and Dad's cars, and how we know that Troy either vandalized them or had someone do it. And, of course, he denied it. But Aaron and Noah chastised Troy and assured me that it wouldn't happen again."

"What about his behavior when he barged into our home?"

"He was told not to ever do that again too," I lied. With everything going on in that meeting earlier, I forgot to mention it. But after eavesdropping on their conversation, hearing Troy say to Noah and Aaron that he would leave me alone after I left the office, that gave me hope that he wouldn't bother me or my family again.

"That's it?"

"Yes, that's it," I told her, and then I said, "Have you ever been around Aaron and Noah and they've said something racist?"

"Of course not. Those are some very diplomatic men. And they do a lot for minority children. So, why do you ask?"

"No reason," I said. I figured that if I told her what I knew that she wouldn't believe me. She had always held Aaron and Noah to a high standard. They could do no wrong in her eyes. So I guess I would just leave well enough alone.

"You're not going to sleep with him tonight, right?"

"Mom, really? What kind of question is that? Of course not!"

"Just checking. Some of the men in this generation are predators, so please be careful and don't stay out all night."

"I won't, Mom, I will come home as soon as we leave the restaurant."

"Glad to hear it," she said, and then she stepped back from my bedroom door and walked away.

* * *

The car Simon instructed to pick me up was parked outside when I walked out of the building. After he opened the door so I could climb inside, he closed it, walked back around the car, climbed in the front seat, and pulled out into the road.

"Can you tell me where we're going?" I asked the white guy.

"I was told to keep it a secret until we get there," he answered while looking at me through the rearview mirror.

I smiled and chuckled. "How did I know that you were going to say that?"

"Then that means that you're a smart woman," he replied.

The drive to the location took twenty-five minutes. When we arrived, I looked up at the sign and realized that we were at Serengeti. I remembered my mother telling me about this place sometime ago. My stepdad brought her here for their fourteenth anniversary. Now I would get to tell her about my own experience here when I returned home.

Immediately after the driver let me out of the car, he escorted me into the restaurant; then from there, the hostess escorted me to the table where Simon was waiting for me. His face lit up as soon as he saw me. I smiled at him as he rose up from his chair. As soon as we got within arm's reach, he hugged me and then pulled out the chair. After I sat down, he pushed my chair back toward the table.

"It's really nice in here," I complimented.

"I'm glad you like it, but the food is much better," he said, and from there, our dialogue began.

"So, how was your day?" he asked. Before I could answer him, our waitress walked up to our table and took our drink order. We also gave her our meal order before she walked away.

"So, are you going to tell me how your day was?" he repeated.

I sighed heavily. "Hectic."

"My day was a little hectic too. But in that situation, you've got to shake it off and keep moving," he advised me.

"How is your relationship with the Weinstein brothers?" I got straight to the point.

"Things are good."

"How long have you known them?"

"For over a decade, I think."

"How did you guys meet?"

"At a fund-raiser. Fund-raisers and annual parties are typically where a lot of the rich folks meet."

"Have you and the Weinstein brothers ever done any business before joining them this time?"

"No. We always talked about it at those events, but I didn't see the need to switch from the corporate counsel I already had. Why do you ask?" He had become curious.

"No reason, really. Just curious is all," I said to him. I wanted to expose the towel Aaron and Noah had placed over his eyes, but I needed to feel him out first. For all I knew, he could step to the Weinstein brothers and blow my cover. Rat me out, more or less.

"How long has your company been in business?"

"Close to seventeen years and it's thriving. But let's cut to the chase. Are you going to take me up on my offer or not?" He didn't mince words. He wanted me to tell him if we were going to see one another in an arranged fashion.

"Umm . . . I don't think I'm ready for that type of relationship."

"What type of relationship do you want to have?"

"Listen, Simon, you seem like a nice guy, but—"

"But she's in a relationship with me," said a voice from behind me.

* * *

I turned around and looked over my shoulder—standing there behind me was Troy.

"What did you just say?" Simon asked him.

"What are you doing here?" I interjected, shaking my head. My mother just warned me that this guy would pop up out of nowhere. What the fuck was wrong with him?

"No, the question is, what are *you* doing here?" he hissed. I saw his teeth grinding against each other.

"Don't answer that. He doesn't own you," Simon barked at Troy.

"And you don't either."

"You're absolutely right. But I could have your ass escorted out of here quicker than you could blink your eyes," Simon threatened him. Simon didn't back down. I could see the balls on him getting bigger by the moment.

"Come on, Yoshi, let's go," Troy instructed me, and grabbed ahold of my arm. He tried to pull me up from the chair, but I resisted.

"I'm not going anywhere with you," I told him, and snatched my arm away from him. And even though I got him to release me, I was worried about what he was going to do next. I didn't know if he'd swing on me or Simon.

"You heard what the lady said. Now leave," Simon told him.

"Make me leave!" Troy tested him as he stood tall, with his chest poking out.

"Is that an invitation?" Simon added.

Troy ignored him and walked from behind and faced me. "Yoshi, I am not leaving here without you." It almost looked like he was begging me. But I wasn't fazed by his apologetic demeanor. Before the office meeting today, he thought I had slept with Simon, and now he knew otherwise. But it's too late. The way he treated me was wrong, and I would never go back to him. And besides, I didn't want his parents turning

over in their graves because he was having an intimate relationship with me. I was done with him, and I was going to
show him.

"Yes, you are," I replied.

"You heard the lady," Simon chimed in.

"Mind your fucking business, dude. She doesn't want your
shriveled-up old ass," Troy snapped.

"Troy, how dare you say that to him?" He was humiliating Simon and me in front of the other guests at the restaurant.

Simon stood up from his chair and flagged the hostess to
get security.

"Troy, you're embarrassing me."

"He's embarrassing both of us," Simon added.

"Yoshi, you didn't sleep with him. It was staged," Troy
started to say. I knew where he was going with this confession, but I just couldn't believe that he was saying it here
and now.

"What are you talking about?!" Simon roared.

"You two didn't fuck. You fell asleep between her legs before you could perform oral sex on her," Troy explained.

I could tell that Simon was confused and taken aback by
Troy's statement, so he rushed up toward Troy like he was
about to hit him. "What do you mean that we didn't have
sex? Were you there?" Simon exploded.

"Come on, you guys, please stop. Everyone in the restaurant is looking at us," I pleaded.

"What is going on here?" a medium-build Caucasian man
asked. He had on a white button-down shirt, with a general
manager name tag pinned to his shirt, with his name placed
underneath it.

"This loser just barged in on our dinner, so he needs to be
escorted out of here," Simon told the general manager.

The general manager turned his attention toward Troy.

"Sir, I can't have you here creating a scene in this restaurant, so I'm going to have to ask you to leave."

"I'll leave, but she's coming with me," Troy told them both, and then he tried to pull me up from the chair.

"Troy, let me go. I am not leaving with you," I reminded him. But he wouldn't release my arm.

"Yoshi, I know that I treated you badly when I thought that you slept with that guy, but I found out today that it didn't happen. You and Simon went to the bedroom, but you both fell asleep before anything happened," he explained again.

"Where did you get that information from?" Simon asked.

"I've seen the video on Aaron's home camera," Troy said.

But I had heard the conversation back at the firm with him, Noah, and Aaron. Troy was lying through his freaking teeth. Aaron told him that he had his private investigator take photos of us. So, if Troy wanted to tell the truth, then tell the real truth. I swear, I wanted to blow the whistle on his ass. But he had already opened a can of worms. When the Weinstein brothers found out that Troy had opened his mouth and said what he had said so far, he might get fired. I guess I would see.

"So, what are you, a stalker and a Peeping Tom?" Simon hissed. I could tell that his blood was boiling.

"Are *you* a fucking Peeping Tom?" Troy replied.

"You know what, I've heard enough. Take his ass out of here!" Simon shouted.

At that very moment, the general manager and another gentleman asked Troy nicely if he'd leave. If not, they would call the cops.

Troy stood there for a second and looked at me. I guess he was waiting for me to tell him that I'd leave with him, but I didn't. I looked away from him, and that was when he knew that I wanted him to leave too.

"So you're really not leaving with me?" he asked.

I turned back around to face him. "You expect me to leave this restaurant after how you treated me earlier in Noah's office? You degraded me with your insults."

"I know, I am sorry."

"Sorry isn't enough. And I have nothing else to say about it," I declared, and then I turned back around in my chair.

"Well, then tell me what to do? Right now, I will do anything to show you how sorry I am," Troy insisted.

I could tell that he was sorry about finding out the real truth behind the situation with Simon. But what if it was true? He wouldn't be apologizing right now. I would still be that same black whore.

"Nothing! You've done enough already," I told him without turning around to face him.

"Come on, sir, let's go," the general manager chimed back in, and then he reached for Troy's arm. Troy snatched his arm away from the guy.

"Don't fucking touch me again, or I'm gonna be forced to defend myself," Troy warned him.

Everyone in attendance knew what that threat meant. The general manager knew it too and pulled out his handheld radio. "Can you get the police here? We have a guest disrupting a paying patron's dinner."

"Do you think I care about the cops? I'm a lawyer and I know my rights!"

"Troy, please leave before they lock you up." This time, I turned just enough to look over my right shoulder.

"No, let him get arrested. Jail is where he belongs. I'm embarrassed that I'm being represented by a firm that he works for," Simon stated.

"Come on, sir, let's get you out of here before the cops get here," the other guy said.

Troy stood there for a second and then he turned around

and walked away. Both men that worked for the restaurant proceeded to walk behind him.

Simon sat back down and began to grill me. "Did you believe what he said?" was his first question.

"I don't know," I replied. But I knew he was telling the truth. What I couldn't believe was that he didn't say more. He, Noah, and Aaron had talked about everything concerning Simon.

"Does Aaron have cameras in his home?" Simon wanted to know.

"Of course, he does. What wealthy person doesn't?" I said while sipping on my cocktail.

"Do you believe him when he said that we didn't have sex?" Simon pressed.

"I can't say. I'm at a loss for words," I replied. But once again, I knew the answer. I heard it come out of the horse's mouth.

"I'm going to give Aaron a call as soon as the firm opens tomorrow morning."

"What are you going to say?"

"I'm going to tell him exactly what Troy told us. And then I'm going to question him about the way he conducts business, because what if what he told us was true? That's an invasion of privacy."

"I agree," I said, and took another sip from my cocktail. I swear, I wanted to tell Simon all of what Troy and I knew about that night, but I was afraid. Since Troy had opened that door, I was going to sit back and see where this situation went.

Simon tried to eat his food, but he couldn't. He'd pick up his fork, play around with the food, and then he'd place the fork back down on his plate.

"You lost your appetite, huh?" I asked between chews of my own food. I hadn't lost my appetite. I was okay. I was actually laughing on the inside, because I knew that Troy had messed up by telling Simon some of the things he knew about that night.

"Yes, I have," he started off saying. "I can't believe that guy came here and ruined our dinner. I come here a lot. The people at this restaurant know me. Do you know how that made me look? Two white men fighting over a black woman?"

"*Two white men fighting over a black woman* . . . What does that mean?" I asked. I was offended by this comment.

"It means everything I just uttered from my lips. It's one thing to argue over a woman in public, but to argue over a black is frowned upon. If any of my business associates saw what just happened, word would spread around town and I would lose a lot of business."

"Are you a racist too?" I snapped. First it was Troy, Aaron, Noah, and now Simon.

"No, I'm not. If I were, I wouldn't be sitting here at this table having dinner with you."

"Then what do you call it?"

"I call it, not allowing *your personal affairs* to spill over into *my business affairs*," he replied nonchalantly.

But I wasn't satisfied. I didn't care how he looked at it, he was playing the race card, and I didn't like it one bit. I stood up from my chair and grabbed my purse, overlapping the chair I was sitting on, and turned around to leave. Simon shot up from his chair and tried to prevent me from going.

"Release my arm," I instructed him.

"Did I just offend you?"

"Of course, you did," I replied, and then I snatched my arm away from him.

"Where are you going?"

"Out of here, and away from you."

He followed me outside of the restaurant. I stood by the curb so I could flag down a taxi.

"Why are you leaving?" he asked.

"Because you are just like Troy, Aaron, and Noah."

He stepped into the street so that he could face me. "What do you mean?" he wanted to know.

"I don't want to discuss that right now," I said as I held my arm out toward the street. There was a taxi coming my way and I wanted to catch it.

"So you're leaving?"

"Yes, I am," I told him, and then before I could blink my eyes, the cab pulled up, I got in, closed the door, and the cab pulled back into the street. I was so happy to get out of there. Dealing with these white guys had become a problem. When I thought that race didn't matter, it reared its ugly head and it came back to bite me.

14

Troy

I cannot believe that bitch chose Simon over me, especially after I apologized. I told her that she and Simon didn't have sex and still she rejected me. If Simon was in arm's reach of me, I knew that I would've kicked his ass. I wanted to beat his ass so bad. How dare he get security to put me out? I knew that I was going to have to do some damage control to Aaron and Noah about my behavior before Simon got them both on the phone. Since I had less than twelve hours to do this, I was going to follow Yoshi's cab back to her place and have a talk with her before she went into her parents' apartment building.

The trip was long going back to her place. Sometimes you get caught up in traffic and sometimes you don't. Tonight was one of those nights when it seemed like it took forever. From the restaurant to her house, it would normally take thirty minutes. This time around, it took ninety minutes. That gave me a lot of time to rehearse what I was going to say to her, and hope that it got me back into her good graces.

As the cab pulled into the valet area of the building, I quickly drove in behind them and hopped out of my car while it was still running. As soon as she stepped up over the curb, I was on her heels. "Yoshi, please talk to me," I began to beg after I managed to walk side by side with her.

"Leave me alone, Troy," she said in a step up from a whisper.

"Just give me a chance to talk to you. I promise I won't take up nothing but two minutes of your time."

She opened the door to the front entrance of the building and went inside. I shot through the door behind her. I skipped by her, cutting her off from moving forward. She knew that I wouldn't make a scene, especially in the lobby of the apartment building, so I used it to my advantage and pulled her into a corner. She snatched her arm away from me after I pulled her out of view from the front counter.

"Look, Yoshi, I am sorry for the way I treated you these last few days."

"Troy, you can keep your *sorry*'s, because I don't want to hear it."

"Will you just listen to me?" I pleaded.

She let out a long sigh. "Go ahead," she agreed.

"After you left Noah's office earlier, they told me that you and Simon didn't have sex. So that meant that he didn't rape you."

"Is that it?" she replied nonchalantly.

"What I'm about to tell you cannot leave this building. It has to stay amongst us." I wanted her to promise me.

"I'm listening."

"Do you promise not to say anything?"

"Yes, I promise."

"While I was in Noah's office earlier, Aaron told me that he staged the whole thing."

"But why?" she asked me.

I hesitated. I knew that I couldn't tell her too much, for fear that she could rat him out. I had a lot to lose, and one word coming from her mouth to Noah and Aaron could ruin me for life.

"Because Aaron wants to keep Simon in his back pocket," I finally answered her.

"What do you mean?"

"He took photos of you guys and intends on using them if Simon ever tries to fire the firm from representation."

"So I take it that I'm in those photos?"

"Yes, you are," I reluctantly replied.

"Have you seen the photos?"

"No, I haven't."

"So, how can you be so sure that there are some?"

"Because I know Aaron. He's like a father to me. He wouldn't lie about something like that."

"So, do you think that it's okay for your father to have photos of Simon and me in bed together?"

"Of course not."

"Well, Troy, you need to get those photos from him," she insisted. "This is your chance to prove to me that you are truly sorry for how you treated me these last couple of days," she added.

"That's going to be hard to do."

"Why is that?"

"Because I don't know where they are."

"They can't be but two places, and that's his office or at his apartment."

"What if they aren't in either place?"

"That's not my problem. It's yours to find out, because this is the only way you can make it up to me."

"What if I can't get my hands on them?"

"Then there's nothing else for us to talk about."

"Do you know that I didn't have to tell you anything about the pictures?"

"Yep, you're absolutely right."

"So give me some slack."

"I don't have to give you shit. You put your hands on me. You disrespected me at the office, in front of the twins, and you disrespected my parents. They told me that you're not allowed in their apartment anymore. So you owe me," she stressed.

"Okay, if I find those photos and give them to you, will you give our relationship another chance?"

"What do you think is going to happen when Simon calls Aaron and tells him what happened tonight?"

"I can't worry about that right now. My main concern is you. I acted like an asshole toward you, and I'm going to do everything I can to make it up to you."

"You know that Aaron and Noah aren't going to allow that."

"I will walk away from the firm and start my own practice if they try to stop us from being together."

"You know they will never let that happen. They pretty much own the city. No one would want you representing them."

"If there is a will, there's a way."

"When did you grow these balls?"

"After you left me. Seeing you with Simon cut me deep in my heart."

"You cut me deep in my heart too, especially when you started calling me a *black whore*, *slut*, and *bitch*. If you love someone, you don't treat them like you did to me."

"I know I did, and that's why I'm going to do everything in my power to make it up to you," I promised. "Will you do me a favor?" I continued.

"What is it?"

"Will you please stop seeing Simon?"

"Not until after you bring me those photos."

"As badly as I want to say no, I know I can't call the shots, so I'm going to get on it now."

"Good, now call me when you get them. And when you get to work tomorrow, I want you to act like we didn't have this conversation. Carry on like we've been doing."

"That's fine. I can do that," I assured her.

"Awesome, now you better get your car before they have it towed," she warned me.

"Oh damn! I forgot about that. Can I get a quick kiss?"

She frowned immediately. "I can't believe that you just asked me that. I'm a *black whore*, right?"

"Come on, Yoshi, you know I was mad."

"I don't care how mad you were. Promise me that you'll never talk to me like that again."

"I promise."

"All right, now get out of here," she said, and that was my cue to leave.

I couldn't stop thinking about Yoshi after I walked away from her. The thought that she was giving me a chance to make things right with her gave me mixed feelings. I wanted to be with her, but then if I did, there was no telling what the senior partners of the firm would do to me. In addition to that, it felt good not to have a bruised heart and ego because of the possibility that Yoshi and Simon slept together. With that out of the way, all I needed to do now was focus on finding those photos and getting to Aaron before Simon did.

As soon as I pulled up to my apartment building, I parked my car and headed into my building. I jumped on the elevator with one of the other tenants and headed up to my floor. The woman got off on the floor two floors underneath me, so when the elevator door closed, I rode the rest of the way alone.

When the elevator let off a *ding* and opened the door, I stepped off on my floor and strolled down the hallway to my apartment. I didn't know why I started humming the melody of "Careless Whisper" by George Michael. Was it because I knew Yoshi had given me a chance of making things right with her? Yes, Aaron and Noah were right; my parents would have forbidden my actions, but my heart ruled and I listened to it.

When I entered my apartment, I hung my car keys up on the key hook on my wall and then I headed down the hallway to my bedroom. Today was definitely an eventful day. So being able to come home, wind down, and collect my thoughts was needed. Immediately after I crossed the entryway of my bedroom, I flipped on the light switch and everything around me went dark. As I felt and heard a loud thudding sound, I knew I had been hit in the back of my head and that I had hit the floor.

At some point later, I squinted my eyes and tried with my arm to shield the light beaming at me. And as my eyes became more and more focused, I saw two guys standing over me. I recognized them immediately. They were the guys that attacked me in the court's parking garage because I hadn't been able to get their boss out of jail by filing for another bail hearing. I swear, I can't tell you how I knew that I was going to die today. The fact that they were able to get into my apartment despite the type of security my apartment building had, I knew that I was doomed.

Before I could utter one word, both men started punching and kicking me in my back and ribs. "You. Think. Somebody. Is. Playing. With. You? You. Still. Haven't. Gotten. Eric. Young. Another. Bail. Hearing." The first guy was speaking and uttered one word with every kick.

"Yeah, he thinks it's a game," said the other guy. His kick had more force behind it.

"I've already set up the court date," I managed to say, trying my best to block any kicks to my head and face. "So please stop!" I begged them.

And what do you know? My lie worked. They both stopped attacking me.

"When is his bail hearing?" the first guy asked.

"In two days," I lied once more.

"What time?" the same guy asked.

"Eleven a.m.," I managed to say. I swear that day and time popped out of the sky.

"You aren't lying to us, are you?" the second guy asked.

"Yeah, you *better not* be lying to us," the first guy stressed.

"Let us see the paperwork," the second guy pressed.

"Yeah, where is the court document? We need to get a copy of it," the other agreed.

"It's not here. It's at my office."

"Then who is the judge?" the first guy asked. He wanted details. I felt like he almost didn't believe me.

"Yeah, who is the judge?" the second guy asked me.

"It's Judge Fallon."

"There's no judge downtown with that last name," the second guy said.

"Yes, there is. He's the magistrate judge in building C."

"You better not be lying to us," the second guy added, and then he kicked me in my back.

BOMB! I swear, that blow to my back sent a sharp pain to my entire body. "Ugggg!" I screamed in agony.

"Shut the fuck up!" the same guy growled, and stomped his foot on my leg with as much force as he could muster up. I buried my mouth into my arm and grunted. If I hadn't done that, I would've been screaming like a rape victim.

"I'm gonna have my girlfriend call the courts in the morning, and if she tells me that there isn't a court date set for Mr. Young, be prepared to die as soon as we see you," the first guy threatened.

"Don't worry. They will confirm the court date I just gave you guys," I tried assuring them both.

"They better" were the last words I heard coming from them, and then they walked out of my apartment, leaving the front door slightly ajar. I struggled to get off the floor, so I crawled to the door and closed it. After I locked it, I just lay there and wondered how I kept getting myself into bullshit. I'd been attacked so many times in these past couple of weeks, it was insane. I knew that if I hadn't given those guys a court date, they would've killed me. Speaking of which, I needed to find out how they got into my apartment. Someone would pay for this.

The following morning, I got up at seven o'clock, showered, got dressed, and before I left my apartment, I called the courts and asked one of the clerks I knew if she could fit me into an eleven o'clock bail hearing for my client. She didn't have an opening for that time, but she was able to get me a 1:00 p.m. slot for that same day.

After I took care of setting the bail hearing for my client, I left my apartment and went to work. I arrived about thirty minutes before my usual time. Natalie, the receptionist, hadn't made it to work, nor had the Weinstein brothers. Two of the firm's juniors were in their offices prepping for court. I waved at both of them as I passed by.

Ryan's office was the next one I passed. "Going to court today?" he asked me.

"I've got a continuance on the docket," I told him, and kept walking.

I proceeded into my office and placed my briefcase down on my desk. I knew that now would be the right time to execute a search in Aaron's office, since he hadn't arrived as of yet. So I took a deep breath, exhaled, and then I shot out of my office.

When I stepped back into the hallway, I looked in both directions to make sure that I was alone. And when I saw that I was, I raced to Aaron's office. The door was closed, but it was unlocked. I entered and closed the door behind me. I rushed over to Aaron's desk and grabbed the drawer knob to pull it open and it wouldn't budge. I shook the knob a couple of times and the drawer would not open. That's when I realized that the drawer was locked. I felt defeated at that very instant.

"The key has to be in the pullout tray right below the desk," I whispered to myself. And what do you know? As soon as I pulled out his long drawer, the key to the other drawers was in view. At that point, I knew that I couldn't waste any time. So I grabbed the key, unlocked the first drawer, and pulled it open. Even though my heart was beating like crazy, I felt a huge amount of relief after I gained entry to this drawer.

Aaron had a lot of files in this drawer, but when I started sifting through them, I miraculously searched the different clients' files and ran across a manila envelope. I shook it and the contents inside led me to believe that there were photos inside, so I opened it. I dug around in the envelope and pulled out the first couple of photos I could grab. Luckily, they were the pictures of Yoshi and Simon. Yoshi was completely naked and so was Simon. The second photo was of Yoshi with her face buried in Simon's lap. The way the photos were captured, they were both naked, in the bed, while Simon's head was tilted back. It looked like he was drowning in ecstasy. I was burning on the inside as I sifted from one picture to the next. I've got to admit that Aaron was a dirty-ass fucker. These photos depicted Yoshi like she and Simon were enjoying one another. These photos could prevent Yoshi from ever trying to sue Aaron or Simon, and it also served as a bargaining chip to keep Simon's mouth shut when he figured out that Aaron was going to rob him when the money started rolling in.

I heard voices coming down the hallway and it alarmed me, so I knew I needed to get out of Aaron's office. I stuffed the photos back into the envelope, and then I stuffed the envelope down the back of my pants. I locked the desk drawer and then I placed the key back in the desk tray.

"Ryan, think your client is going to accept the plea deal?" I heard Noah say, and I immediately stood straight up. My adrenaline started pumping like crazy. My anxiety level went through the roof.

"Come on, Troy, you gotta get out of here," I warned myself softly.

"I think he will. If he doesn't, then he's up shit's creek," I heard Ryan say.

"Good luck!" I heard Noah reply.

This time, his voice was closer. His office was next to Aaron's, so I knew that he had to pass by here to get to his office. If I got caught in Aaron's office, I would have to do a lot of explaining. And even if I came up with a plausible story, Aaron and Noah would pick it apart and I'd probably be sanctioned.

As Noah's voiced traveled, I hid behind Aaron's door until Noah passed. I swear, I had never sweated more quickly than I was doing now. Once Noah passed Aaron's office, I managed to open the door quickly and quietly, then slipped out before anyone could catch me. Instead of going in the direction of Noah's office, which was right next door, I walked back in the direction I came. Ryan wasn't in his office, but the other junior partner was. He was looking through files in his five-foot metal cabinet, so his back was facing the entrance of his office; he didn't see me when I passed by his office.

I exhaled a sigh of relief that I did not get caught inside of or leaving Aaron's office. With Yoshi and Simon's photos in my possession, I strolled into my office and stuffed them inside of my briefcase. The thought of having them was a bittersweet feeling; what if Aaron came to work and looked for them and couldn't find them? It wouldn't shock me if he locked down the floor and had everyone and everything searched. If he did that, shit would hit the fan. I could only hope that didn't happen.

Aaron eventually came to work around 9:00 a.m. He always walked the entire floor to greet everyone and to make them aware that he was in the building, so they better stay on their toes.

When he passed by my office, I pretended to be on the phone so he would only acknowledge me via a wave and keep walking. Turned out, that's exactly what he did. But then after he walked by, I realized that I needed to tell him what had happened at last night's dinner between Simon and Yoshi, but what if Simon got a chance to call and give his personal account first? So I got back up from my seat, peered around the corner of the entryway of my door, and watched as Aaron casually walked to his office.

"Hey, Aaron, can I talk to you for a moment?" I got up the gumption to say.

Aaron stopped and turned around. "Sure, son, come on to my office," he said. After getting the green light from Aaron, I stepped into the hallway, closed my door shut, and then headed in his direction.

Aaron walked into his office first and I followed. "Turn on that light switch and have a seat," he instructed as he continued to his desk.

I flipped the light switch and then took a seat in one of the chairs placed in front of his desk. He placed his briefcase on the floor next to his desk, and then gave me his undivided attention.

"So, what do you want to talk about?" he asked me.

I was nervous about what I was about to reveal to him, and how he was going to take it. My only hope for this conversation was that I didn't get fired.

"Have you spoken to . . ." I started off saying, but then Aaron's office phone rang.

"Hold that thought," he said, and then he picked up the phone receiver. "This is Aaron," he announced to the caller, and then he fell silent.

Watching Aaron converse with whoever was on the telephone took my anxiety to another level, especially after looking at me a couple of times while the caller was talking. "Okay, thanks for letting me know," he added, and then hung up.

At that very moment, I knew that Simon was the caller, so what I needed to do was damage control. I needed to give Aaron my side of things and make it look like I was the victim, not Simon.

"That was Yoshi on the phone. She said that she was sick and that she needed to take off today. Does that have anything to do with you?" he asked.

Hearing that Yoshi was the caller made my heart fall into the pit of my stomach. I instantly wondered why she wanted to take today off. Was it because I embarrassed her last night and she didn't want to face me? Or could it be that she didn't want to make things awkward while we were both at work today? Whatever it was, I needed to get to the bottom of it.

"No, it has nothing to do with me," I lied. I knew it had everything to do with me.

"Well, then, tell me what you want to talk about?"

I attempted to answer his question, but my mind was deadlocked. Should I tell Aaron or not about last night? I figured that if I did, I would be blowing the whistle on myself after Aaron realized that the photos of Simon and Yoshi were gone. But then, what if Simon called this morning and released the floodgates about what happened last night? This situation was a bad one. And I did not know how to maneuver around it.

"Spit it out," he pressured me.

"I just wanted to know if I had a chance of becoming a senior partner?" I finally said. I swear, this was the only thing I could think to say.

Aaron chuckled. "Is that it?"

I chuckled too. "Yeah," I replied.

"How long have you been a junior partner?"

"Two years now."

"Give it another year and then the other senior partners will discuss it."

"All right, sounds good to me," I said, and then I stood up from the chair and exited Aaron's office.

Instead of going back into my office, I walked by it and headed for the elevator. Natalie was sitting at her desk when I walked by. She spoke to me, but I ignored her. Through my peripheral vision, I saw her roll her eyes, but I let it slide. I had bigger fish to fry.

When the elevator door opened, I got on it and took it to the lobby. There were three telephones located on the first-floor lobby. They were there for the purpose of visitors to call and alert the patron that they had arrived and were waiting. I grabbed the first phone in my reach. It was next to the first-floor restroom.

"Yoshi, please answer," I uttered quietly.

Thankfully, she answered the call on the third ring.

"Hello," she said.

"Hey, don't hang up. It's me, Troy," I told her.

"Where are you calling me from?"

"I'm in the first-floor lobby."

"Didn't I tell you not to call me until you have the pictures?"

"I got them."

"I don't believe you."

"I do. I've got them in my briefcase in my office."

"How did you get them?"

"They were hidden in Aaron's desk drawer of his office."

"How were you able to do that?"

"I snuck into his office before he came in."

"What are you going to do if he calls a meeting and addresses the fact that an envelope of photos were taken from his office?"

"That's one of the reasons why I called you."

"Let me hear it."

"First of all, why did you call in sick? I was in Aaron's office when you called in for a sick day."

"Because I needed some time home to figure things out. So, if I had come to work, I wouldn't have been able to do that."

"Well, I need you to come here and pick up the photos."

"I just called in sick. How do you think it's going to look if I come there?"

"I can meet you here in the lobby."

"I don't know about that, Troy. That sounds risky."

"I know it does, but that's the only way I can get rid of it without leaving the building."

Yoshi fell silent.

"Yoshi, I thought that you wanted the photos?"

"I do."

"Well, then act like it."

She fell silent again.

"Yoshi, please. I need you to do this."

"All right, give me an hour and I'll call you from the lobby's phone when I arrive."

After Yoshi agreed to meet me, I raced back upstairs to my office, hoping that Aaron or Noah wasn't looking for me. Aaron was someone that would go to the men's restroom to find me, but Noah would just wait until I came from wherever I'd been.

When I exited the elevator, Natalie was on a call with one of the firm's clients. I didn't acknowledge her, and she didn't acknowledge me. As I made my way to my office, I met Noah in the hallway. He was just leaving Aaron's office.

"Aaron is looking for you," he informed me.

Just hearing the words *Aaron* and *looking* sent me into a tailspin of trepidation. But I kept a brave face.

"Is he in his office now?" I asked Noah, even though I already knew the answer.

"Yes, he's in there now," he replied as he passed by me.

As much as I dreaded seeing Aaron right now, I knew that I had to find out what he wanted with me. The only thing I could think of: the fucking photos. What if he knew that I had them? But how could he? There were no cameras in his office. Not even in the hallways. But I guess I would find out.

Before I went to Aaron's office, I made a short detour to my office. I needed to make sure that those photos were still in my possession. When I entered my office, I noticed that my briefcase hadn't been moved, so I was relieved that no one had been in my office. But I still needed to make sure that they were in the place where I put them. Without hesitation, I opened my briefcase and was instantly relieved when I saw that the photos were still in the spot where I placed them. Now I could go and face Aaron and hope that he was not onto me.

I approached his office door and knocked on it. He looked up from his desktop computer.

"Hey, son, where were you?" was his first question.

"I was in the coffee room," I replied while standing at the entryway of his office. "Can I come in?" I asked him.

"Yes, of course. Come on in and take a seat," he insisted.

And, boy, was my heart rate racing, all while trying to figure out why he was looking for me.

"So, what's up?" I asked.

"Are you all right?" he wanted to know. He had a legitimate reason for asking me that question because I was acting all paranoid.

"Oh yeah, I'm fine," I tried to assure him.

"Are you sure?"

"Yes, I'm sure."

"Okay, well, if you insist," he replied, and then he said, "Are you going to seek charges against the guys that attacked you?"

"I haven't decided as of yet."

"Well, I think you should. You just can't let hoodlums bang you up because you didn't make something happen for them in court."

"Yeah, I know."

"If you want me to get our boys on it, I will. That way, we can keep your hands clean." Aaron smiled.

"No one would get killed, right?" I asked. Aaron and Noah were powerful men. They knew people who were philanthropists to gangsters. They were nothing to play with.

Aaron chuckled. "Of course not," he said, and then he winked his eye at me. I knew what that meant. "Troy, we can't have clients sending their goons to beat up attorneys because their court cases didn't end in their favor. We have to make examples out of them."

"Yeah, I agree," I answered, and then Aaron's office phone started ringing. Once again, my nerves started rattling. The palms of my hands started sweating profusely. I was helpless and I needed to get on the other side of this, so I watched Aaron's facial expression.

"This is Aaron," he said into the phone. "Oh sure, send him back," he added, and then he hung up the call.

"That was my nine o'clock appointment," he said, and then he looked down at his wristwatch, which was the presidential Rolex Day-Date. "Time goes by so fast," he continued.

Relieved, I stood up from my seat. "Well, let me let you get to it."

"Let's talk about that thing later," he insisted.

"Yeah, let's do that," I replied, and exited his office.

15
Yoshi

I was nervous as hell to walk back in the building when I took a sick day. I couldn't help but look over my shoulder with every step I took. As soon as I laid eyes on a telephone, I rushed over there and called Troy's desk.

"Are you here?" he asked after he answered and I told him it was me.

"Yes, I'm here," I replied.

"Be down there in a second."

"Okay, see you then."

I sat down in a lounge chair in the lobby a few feet from the telephone I used to call Troy. Once I felt like no one was onto me, I relaxed a little. While I waited for Troy to meet me, I looked down at my wristwatch at least a dozen times. I can honestly say that I know how someone committing a crime feels. I was on pins and needles. I grabbed a *People* magazine and started sifting through the pages. Doing this was the distraction I needed. After looking at photos of Hollywood celebrities in the first ten pages, Troy showed up. He walked up behind me.

"Come on, let's go outside," he said after he leaned in toward me. He made it apparent that he didn't want anyone to hear him but me.

I stood up on my feet. "Where are we going?" I whispered after I leaned in toward him.

"Outside," he replied, and grabbed ahold of my hand.

I followed him as he led the way. I held my head down just in case someone from the firm walked by us.

As soon as Troy and I walked outside, he pulled a manila envelope from his suit jacket and handed it to me. I looked at the front and back of the envelope and it was blank. "There's nothing written on this," I stated.

"That's how I found it. But trust me, it's the pictures. Now put 'em in your purse before someone sees it."

I took his instructions and stuffed the envelope into my purse. "Did you look at all of them?" I wondered aloud.

"No, I only looked at a couple of them. After I saw the third one, I put the rest of them away. It was hard to look at you in bed with another man," he explained. I could see the hurt in his eyes. But hell! *I* was the fucking victim. In the beginning, he thought I wanted to fuck Simon; so at this point, I wasn't concerned with his feelings. He disrespected me and he assaulted me, so I have no tears to shed for him.

"I've been waiting for Simon to call the office. So far, he hasn't done that."

"That's what I was going to talk to you about."

"What is it?"

"I talked to him last night. I told him I would give him the photos if he wouldn't call Aaron," I shared.

"That's it? You're giving the photos just like that? What do you get out of the deal?"

"Nothing," I lied. I had to give Troy the impression that I

was doing this trade-off for him, and not for me. "I'm doing this for you," I added.

"What if he calls Aaron anyway? Do you know what that would do to me? Aaron would have me locked up for going through his things in his office."

"No, he can't."

"Yes, he can. And it's called *petty larceny*. On top of that, I would lose my job, and after they blackball me, I would never be able to practice law in the state of New York."

"He's not going to tell Aaron."

"Get copies *before* you give him the originals," Troy stressed.

"Okay, if you insist."

"I'm trying to look out for us both."

"Trying to look out for us both should've happened when I confided in you—and you believed me."

Troy looked around our surroundings and then looked back at me. "When are you supposed to meet Simon?"

"Around noon," I told him.

Troy looked down at his watch. "You have two hours. Where are you two meeting?"

"At his office."

"No, call him back and tell him to meet you somewhere in public. Like a diner or a bookstore. Yeah, tell him to meet you at the Barnes and Noble not too far from here."

"What's wrong with his office? That's a public place."

"Just do what I tell you. Call him back and tell him to meet you at the Barnes and Noble."

I sucked my teeth. This asshole thought he still controlled me. He missed the mark on that when he put his freaking hands on me.

"Yeah, okay," I told him, and then I turned to leave.

He grabbed my arm. "Wait, I don't get a kiss?"

I looked back at him and then I looked down at his hand. "Do you think you deserve one?"

"Can I get a thank-you at least?"

"Thank you," I said, and then he released my arm. "Don't call me. I'll call you."

"Okay."

I walked back to the parking garage to pick up my car, and I saw something move through my peripheral vision. Before I turned to see who it was, everything around me went black. I screamed after realizing that someone had thrown a Velcro-fastened bag over my head.

"Somebody help!"

"Shut the fuck up before I kill you right here," a man growled.

"Okay. Okay. I won't say anything else. Just please don't kill me," I begged.

Instead of assuring me that he wouldn't, the guy instructed me to get in the backseat of a car. And when I did, he told me to lie down on the backseat. So I did.

Moments later, I heard another voice, in addition to the one that had instructed me to do everything. In total, there were two guys. So, as I heard the tires squeal and the engine revving, I knew that I had been kidnapped, and that I was about to enter an underworld that some women never resurface from.

I lay there quietly, trying to figure out what they were going to do with me. But every time I tried to come up with an answer, my mind drew a blank. So I lay there and started praying.

During the course of the drive, no one said anything. But they did play music from a local radio station. I couldn't say if it was because they didn't want me to hear the noise outside of the car or because they were told not to talk. Either way, I was still in the dark.

The driver finally stopped the car after turning four corners and drove down a steep incline. When they opened their doors, that's when they started speaking.

"Grab her and follow me," I heard the driver say. The guy escorting me with a firm grip of my arm obliged and did what he was instructed to do.

"Let's go," he said, and I followed.

We walked for about twenty feet and then we walked onto an elevator. Both men were still silent while one operated the elevator. I wanted to say something so bad, but I was afraid that they might assault me or, even worse, kill me, so I cooperated with them and did everything they told me to do.

The elevator door opened a minute and a half later and we exited it.

"Come this way," the driver said.

The guy escorting me didn't say another word until a door opened and closed.

"Sit," he instructed me as he guided me to sit down without falling onto the floor.

I sat there quietly, wondering what was going to happen next. And before my mind kicked into high gear, the bag was lifted from my head. I found myself squinting due to sudden light in the room. After I refocused my vision, I realized that I was in an old office inside of an old warehouse. And standing in front of me were four guys dressed in suits. They were the two kidnappers, and now two new people. All four were Caucasian men. Intimidation and fear for my life flooded my entire soul. I wanted to ask them not to kill me, but I was too afraid to open my mouth.

"I know you're wondering why you're here?" the guy in the middle said.

"Yes, that would be my first question," I replied. But I knew who they were. Their attire spoke volumes to me. And with the back-to-back physical attacks on Troy for his shady business deals and gambling debts, I knew there was a possibility that I could be used as target practice: an eye opener for

Troy, with hopes that he'd take care of the business he'd done around town.

The guy who appeared to be head of their organization took a couple of steps toward me and said, "We're the FBI. My name is Special Agent Petty. Agent Gemma is the guy that took the bag from your head. Agent Shein was the driver, and this guy standing next to me is Agent Hynes."

"What do you want from me? I haven't committed any crimes," I said boldly after finally realizing that they weren't about to murder me.

"You're absolutely right. But you do serve a purpose."

"What kind of purpose is that?" I wondered aloud. I wanted to know where this guy was going with this conversation.

"You're here to talk to us about the Weinstein brothers."

"What about them?" I asked, my confidence was growing faster and faster.

"We're investigating two murders. And we believe that the Weinstein brothers had their hands in it."

I chuckled. "You think that they're involved in a murder?"

"Yes, we do."

"So, why aren't you arresting them, instead of kidnapping me? Do you know that when your agents placed that bag over my head and threw me in the back of a car, I almost pissed on myself? I literally thought that they were going to kill me, and that's not a good feeling to have."

"I want to apologize for that. But we had to do it that way because we didn't want to take the chance of you not coming if we asked. We also didn't want to give you a chance to call Troy."

"Never mind all of that, what do you want from me?"

"We want the photos of you and Simon."

"They're in my purse, and Agent Gemma over here has my purse."

Agent Gemma dug inside of my handbag, retrieved the manila envelope, and handed them to Special Agent Petty.

"What's the significance behind the photos?" I wanted to know.

"I'll explain that part later. But for now, let's talk about these murders."

"When were these two people murdered?"

"About a year ago."

"Well, if it's been that long, then I don't think that I can help you. I just started working there two months ago."

"We know when you started interning there."

"So tell me, what's going on? You're stressing me out with this shit. First I get involved with Troy, then he starts physically assaulting me because he thought that I slept with Simon. On top of that, he goes to my parents' house and acts a complete fool, insulting my parents. Disrespecting them. It was a mess. And now you come to me with this BS. You just don't understand how much stress I've endured these last couple of weeks. I didn't ask for this shit. It just fell in my lap. So tell me how to fix it and be done with it?"

Special Agent Petty looked at Agent Gemma and said, "Has our mole entered the building yet?"

"He just did," Agent Gemma confirmed.

"Fetch him for me," Petty instructed.

Everyone in the room fell silent. Even I didn't say another word, watching my surroundings and everyone's movements. I wanted to know what was about to happen after seeing Agent Gemma leave the room.

About forty seconds later, he reappeared and he wasn't alone. Simon was with him.

My mouth dropped wide open. I couldn't fucking believe it. Was Simon a freaking FBI agent?

As he walked toward me, he tried to hold his head down,

trying to avoid eye contact with me, but I wasn't having it. I wanted him to look at me and see the mess he'd put me in.

"Don't look down. Look at me!" I snapped.

He looked at me briefly and then he turned his focus toward Special Agent Petty.

"What the fuck is going on?" I asked as I looked at Simon, and then shifted my attention toward Special Agent Petty.

"No, Simon isn't an FBI agent. He is our mole. He works for us on the side."

"You mean *snitch*?"

Special Agent Petty and Agent Gemma both chuckled, but Agent Gemma spoke up. "She and I are on the same page with that one."

"Can I get some answers here?" I asked, growing increasingly frustrated by the second.

Special Agent Petty turned his attention toward Simon and instructed him to tell me what was going on.

"I was arrested for ten counts of wire fraud over a year ago, and instead of going to federal prison, I opted to help these guys here building a case against the Weinstein brothers for two counts of murder."

"Who is it that they murdered?"

"A fellow by the name of David Crosley, and another fellow by the name of Dan Eisen."

"When were they murdered?" I asked him, but Simon pointed toward Special Agent Petty to take over the conversation.

"A year ago, those two guys went missing after attending the Weinsteins' annual party. It has been brought to our attention that those guys have what you would call a *secret brotherhood*. They are called the Dragons. And every year they get together on that night, wearing their black robes and create a cleansing. The cleansing is a sacrifice of ordinary people from the streets or someone they know and hate. You name it, those people are the targets. So we put Simon in the fold. He's attending that annual party, and while he's there, he will be recording everything and help us gain entry into this place."

"Seems like you have all of your bases covered. So, why am I here?"

"Because you will be Simon's guest. You will assist him."

"What about Troy? Does he have a part in this?"

"No, he doesn't."

"So, why didn't you ask him to help Simon?"

"Because he's not trustworthy."

"So, wait, why did you want the photos?"

"Because we don't want them getting into the wrong hands."

"So it's true then?"

"What?"

"That he and I didn't have sex."

"Yes, that's correct. See, Aaron spiked your drinks, which was why he was able to get you two asleep, so that he could get some shots of you both in vulnerable positions. This is a common practice of his."

"I know. I was eavesdropping on their conversation after I left their office yesterday."

"We know all about it."

"How?"

"Because while the Weinstein brothers have wiretaps in some of the rooms in that office, we have ours too."

"So, if you have it, then you should know who killed those guys."

"We couldn't get the wiretaps installed until months after those guys went missing. By then, no one has talked about it."

"You do know that this party is a couple of days away. They moved it up because they're going to a golf tournament."

"We're already on it," Special Agent Petty assured me.

I sat there and tried to digest everything that was just fed to me. I couldn't wrap my head around Simon being a fucking snitch. I also couldn't wrap my head around the Weinsteins being involved in a murder.

"Hey, wait, I just remembered something," I blurted out.

"What is it?"

"I remember hearing Troy tell Noah and Aaron that he would take care of me. Meaning, that could be a code word for *kill*, right?"

Special Agent Petty looked at Agent Hynes and said, "Did you pick that up on the scanner?"

"I'll have to check it."

"Are you sure you heard Troy say it?" Special Agent Petty wanted assurance.

"Yes, I heard Troy say it, and Aaron gave him the green light."

"Well, that changes things, because if Troy has invited you to the party, then that means that you're his sacrificial lamb."

"We're gonna have to give Simon an escort," Gemma interjected.

"Who's available at the department?" Petty wondered aloud.

"Agent Tracy isn't working a case right now," Gemma replied.

"Okay, she's perfect. We will get Simon to escort her, while Yoshi mingles around on the floor," Petty stated.

"Look, I know you guys are making last-minute plans for this party, but can I ask Simon something?" I interjected.

"Sure," Petty agreed.

I looked directly at Simon. This time, he held his head up and waited for me to say what it was that I had to say. "Everything you said to me about putting me up in a penthouse, buying me a new car, and giving me a weekly allowance, was that all a ruse?"

He nodded his head, indicating that it was all a lie, so I looked at Special Agent Petty. "Damn, now that's really messed up, because I was looking forward to getting a weekly allowance," I commented.

Every agent in the room burst into laughter.

"Aren't you relocating to Miami?" Special Agent Petty asked me.

"Yes."

"So, don't you think that would've interfered with your weekly allowance?"

"Yes, I thought about that. And that's why I was going to sell him those photos that Aaron's private eye took of us."

All of the agents laughed again.

"She's a smart cookie," Petty complimented me.

"Yeah, she is," Gemma agreed.

"All right, you guys, let's wrap this up," Special Agent Petty announced, and then he clapped his hands together. "Agent Gemma, you and Shien take Ms. Lomax back to her car. Agent Hynes, you and Simon come with me. We've got to do some last-minute planning," he continued to say as they followed him in the opposite direction.

"What about me? What am I supposed to do until the night of the party?" I shouted.

"Just go on as usual and keep this meeting confidential. Don't even mention it to your best friend or college buddies. And please don't mention any of this to your parents. And if we need you for anything else, we know how to contact you."

"Can I make a suggestion?"

"Sure."

"No more kidnapping."

Special Agent Petty smiled. "You got it," he said, and then he kept moving.

* * *

The FBI agents dropped me back off where they had picked me up from. This time around, they had some car etiquette and said good-bye before they left me standing next to my Honda Prelude.

I visually searched the garage, and when I was sure that no one was watching me or hanging around, I climbed in and jetted out of there. While en route to my parents' house, I couldn't stop thinking about what had just transpired. Simon was a freaking FBI informant and the Weinstein brothers were murderers. Who would've thought? What had I gotten myself into?

I should've known that something was wrong when Troy volunteered and elected himself to take care of me at their annual party games. I guess, it didn't register to me that those guys acted and played the roles of gods. That was scary to me. In my mind, they were devil worshipers. Only evil dwelled with evil. And I didn't want any part of it.

When I made it home, I called my best friend, Maria. I felt like a weight was lifted when I told my parents that I wanted to move to Florida, and now that I had their blessing, I figured that now I could tell Maria the good news.

"Maria, you are not going to believe it" was the first thing I said after she answered her telephone.

"What?" she replied.

"I told my parents about moving to Florida and they're on board."

"That's awesome. So, when are you coming?"

"I'm going to give the firm I work with a couple of weeks' notice and then I'm out of here."

"What about your boyfriend? Is he on board too?"

"His opinion doesn't matter, because we just parted ways."

"Sorry to hear that."

"Don't be. I figure it's better this way. I'm sure if we were still together, he'd try to stop me from leaving."

"You have a point there," she agreed. "What about the bar exam that's coming up?"

"I'm not going to take it. I'm going to come to Florida and study for their bar exam and pray that I pass."

"You will. I'm going to help you."

"Maria, you're the freaking best."

"Don't mention it. But in the meantime, I'm going to find out the date for the next bar exam and then I'll call you and let you know."

"Perfect."

"You know you have the option of staying with me until you find a place."

"I appreciate that."

"That's what friends do. So let me get off this phone. I've got a lunch date and I don't want to keep him waiting because I'm not dressed yet."

"Have fun."

"I will. And I look forward to talking to you soon."

"Same here," I said, and then I ended the call.

"Yes, one thing down and two things left to cross off my list," I said to myself, and smiled.

Even though I was in good spirits after talking to Maria, I wanted so badly to tell her about the mess I'd been dragged into. But I couldn't. Per Special Agent Petty, I couldn't open my mouth and tell no one about what was going on amongst the FBI Agents, Simon, and the Weinstein brothers. It was all a big ball of evilness. Something I thought I would never have been involved with. I tell you what, I could probably deal with it better if I got me a line of coke from somewhere. But where? I knew no one that sold drugs. I was a kid born with a silver spoon in my mouth, living uptown with the rich people. So, where could I get my hands on some product?

I got in my car and took a drive to Harlem. I drove up to 142nd Street and Saint Nick Avenue. I remember as a child coming to this part of New York. I didn't know it at first, but my dad used to come here and buy drugs. I knew that I wouldn't run into the same people that sold drugs to him. I'm sure that generation was long gone, but I knew that I would run into someone that would let me do business with them.

As expected, I didn't see any old faces, but a group of younger Dominican guys allowed me to purchase a hundred dollars' worth of coke from them. I was leery when I approached them, but they made me feel like a homegirl and gave me no problems. I was back on the road again, heading in the direction of my parents' apartment. This could not have been a better feeling. It was a huge relief for me to have something in my hands that would help me take my mind off the fact that I was helping a group of FBI agents find evidence of two murders that the Weinstein brothers were involved in during a sacrificial cult cleansing. I swear, I couldn't get home fast enough.

As soon as I walked back into the apartment, I headed straight to my bedroom, locked my door, and retired for the rest of the day.

16
Troy

I've had several meetings with Aaron and Noah these past couple of days and there's been no mention of the missing photos, until now, at the staff meeting. Everyone from the senior partners to the interns and the mailroom workers congregated in the conference room to go over the firm's to-do list and productivity evaluations for the week. So that meant Yoshi was front and center. I tried to avoid eye contact with her the entire time. Aaron took the floor and everyone gave him their undivided attention.

"For this week's announcements, I want to let you guys know that we just signed up a couple of new clients, that means more money for me," he started off saying, and then everyone in the meeting, including him, chuckled.

"What about me?" Noah chimed in.

"You already have more money than me," Aaron joked.

"Don't believe that, you guys," Noah added, looking at everyone in the room.

The entire staff burst into more laughter.

"Moving along, for those that didn't see the flyers on the community board in our café room, our annual party has moved up, so that a few of us senior partners can attend a golfing tournament. And no, we don't have any extra seats on the company's jet. I'm talking to you, Troy," Aaron added, and chuckled.

The entire room burst into laughter again.

"Okay, so it's been brought to my attention that someone is rummaging through other people's belongings and walking out of their offices with things that don't belong to them. We've never had this problem before, so let's end it now before it gets any worse. Now, to the person that took some things that didn't belong to them, please return it or leave it in the common area of this firm. We are family here. Let's not turn it into something else. It would break my heart if we have to make changes around here."

Everyone murmured amongst themselves.

"I have more sad news," he continued. "It has been brought to our attention that Yoshi won't be taking the New York State Bar Exam. She will be relocating to Florida and continuing on with her endeavors there. So, at this year's annual party, we will celebrate the time she has spent with us and send her off in style," Aaron announced, and then he looked over at Yoshi, smiled at her, and clapped his hands along with everyone else in the room.

Yoshi looked at me strangely, because she didn't tell Aaron that she was leaving the firm to relocate to Florida. I did.

"Okay, so I guess this concludes our weekly meeting. Now let's get to work," he stated, and then he turned his attention toward me. "Noah and I want to talk to you a minute," he said, only loud enough for me to hear. And believe me, I knew what it was about.

* * *

After the room emptied out, I sat there with compunctions erupting in the pit of my stomach, knowing full well what Aaron and Noah were going to talk to me about. I tried everything within my power to be cool, calm, and collected.

I smiled at them both. "Are we about to talk about a raise?" I asked, and then I chuckled nervously.

"I don't want to play cat-and-mouse games with you, so I'm gonna get to the point," Aaron stated.

"I'm all ears," I said plainly, trying to be as straight-forward as I could.

"Where are the photos of Simon and Yoshi?" Aaron didn't hesitate to say.

"You're asking the wrong guy. I don't have them," I told him, being as sincere as I could.

"Cut the crap, Troy! Aaron and I know that you have them," Noah interjected.

"I don't. Really, I don't," I denied.

"Then where are they?" Aaron chimed back in.

"I don't know."

"You know I could have your ass for this?" Aaron warned me.

"But I don't have them. Maybe someone else has them. Check with the cleaning crew that cleans after we leave."

"Troy, why are you doing this? You are like our son," Noah said.

"I know. And that's why I wouldn't do anything like that to you guys."

"Cut the crap, Troy! And tell us where the fucking photos are!" Aaron roared, and slammed his fist on the conference table.

"I told you that I don't have them."

"But you are the only person, besides Noah and my private investigator, that knows that they exist," Aaron reminded me.

"Have you even asked your PI guy about them?" I said, trying to shift the blame.

"Noah, do you hear this bullshit?" Aaron said, and shook his head. I could tell that he was growing tired of me. He knew I had the photos, but there was no way that I was going to admit to it.

"Troy, we know that you have the photos, so just give them back to us and we'll forget all about having this conversation," Noah pleaded with me.

But once again, I was not going to admit to taking anything out of Aaron's office, especially those photos. Noah said that they would sweep it underneath the rug, but that's straight bullshit. If I told them that I took the photos, they would find something else on me and fire my ass next week. I may be bipolar, but I am not naïve.

"So you're gonna pretend and lie to us about not having the photos, right?" Aaron asked me again.

"If I had them, I would give them to you."

"Does Yoshi have them?" Noah blurted out.

"Yeah, did you take them and give them to Yoshi?" Aaron inquired.

"No."

"So, if I call Yoshi into this conference room right now and ask her if she knows the whereabouts of those photos, she's gonna tell me that she doesn't know?" Aaron's questions continued.

Caught between a rock and a hard place, I had to make a decision—a decision that would make Yoshi culpable of taking the photos versus myself. But I needed a plausible way to explain it to Noah and Aaron.

"Okay, check it out. Yoshi is the one that took the photos. And she took them because I slipped up and told her in an argument that I had proof of her cheating on me. Now I can get them back, that is no problem. And if you give me a chance, I can trick her into giving them to me."

"And how do you propose to do that?" Aaron asked me.

"I'm gonna be nice to her and act like I'm not upset with her anymore. Trust me, she'll fall right back under my spell," I told him.

Aaron and Noah looked at one another. They saw right through my bullshit. But what other choice did they have? I held the cards to deal with Simon.

"I want those photos in my hands by the night of the annual event," Aaron ordered.

"I can do that," I assured him.

"Don't forget that you gave us your word that you're gonna take part in the cleansing."

"Yes, I gave my word to you two, so I stand on it."

"Good, because your life depends on it," Aaron replied with finality.

After the meeting with Noah and Aaron, I went back to my office and thought long and hard how I was going to get those photos back from Yoshi. She had to know that they were looking for them because of the announcement Aaron made at the meeting. I just hoped that after we gave him those photos back, things would fall into place and I could get back in the good graces of the senior partners.

Needing to empty my bladder, I headed to the men's restroom. En route, I walked by the office that Yoshi shared with Jillian. While Jillian wasn't looking, I waved Yoshi to follow. She waited a couple of minutes and then followed me. Once inside, I locked the door and drilled her with one question after the next.

"Did anyone see you come in here?"

"No."

"What did you do with the photos?"

"I put them away. Why?"

"You heard what he said in the weekly meeting. He wants the photos back," I told her.

"Does he know that I have them?" she asked.

"No, he doesn't. He believes that I took them and just wants me to give them back to him," I denied. I couldn't tell her that I placed most of the blame on her. She'd cave in and tell both Noah and Aaron the truth. I had too much invested in this firm to allow her to destroy it. "So, where are they?"

"I put them in a safety-deposit box."

"Well, I'm gonna need you to get them back. Aaron is giving me until the night of the annual party to put them back in his hands, so please don't screw this up."

"What would happen if I mysteriously lose them?" Yoshi wondered aloud.

"Is that what you wanna do?"

"It was just a what-if?"

"He'll make things really hard for the both of us."

"Well, since I'm leaving really soon, I guess it wouldn't affect me, huh?"

"Don't be mad. It just slipped out of my mouth."

"Well, the next time you slip up and tell them something about my business, I'm gonna slip up and tell them some of yours," she said, and slapped me on my arm. "I'm out of here before I get caught talking to you," she added, and then left the restroom.

17

Yoshi

This week's meeting in the conference room, led by Aaron and Noah, scared the shit out of me. I wasn't the one that stole the photos out of Aaron's office, but I had them in my possession, until I handed them off to the feds. Now what the hell was I going to do? I couldn't go back to Special Agent Petty and tell him that Aaron knew the photos were missing and wanted them back, or could I?

I couldn't tell Troy that I gave the photos to the feds. If I did that, I would have to explain to him why they had them, which would eventually lead me to telling him that Simon was an informant. And this whole thing would blow up in everyone's faces. Simon would be exposed and the feds' investigation of those two men that were murdered a year ago would go up in smoke. I couldn't have that.

I could see the articles now in the *New York Times* and the *New York Post*: *A one- year-old murder investigation headed by the FBI collapsed. It fell apart due to a sex scandal be-*

*tween an intern at Weinstein and Weinstein Law Firm and
CEO Simon Howard, a building/development entrepreneur
turned FBI informant.* It would be a freaking disaster, and it
would devastate my parents. I needed to get Special Agent
Petty on the telephone, and I meant ASAP.

It seemed like I watched the clock on the wall all day, and
five o'clock could not have gotten here any faster. Instead of
getting in my car and going straight home, I drove across
town and stopped at the gas station. I needed gas for my car
and I needed to use the pay phone in the same parking lot as
the service station, so I utilized them both.

My first priority was to call Petty, and that's what I did.
He wasn't in the office, but my call was transferred to Agent
Gemma. I told him what had happened at the meeting today
and that I needed to get those photos back. However, after
speaking with him, I was told that it would be impossible.

Before I got off the phone with Agent Gemma, he put me
in contact with Agent Tracy by transferring my call to her
desk.

"Hi, Yoshi, this is Agent Tracy," she introduced herself.

"Hi, ma'am," I replied.

"So I hear that you want those photos back."

"Yes, I do. We had a weekly meeting today and Aaron
knows that those pictures were taken out of his office."

"That's unfortunate. But we've already put those photos
in evidence, so we don't have access to them right now."

"Do you know when you could get them? See, our annual
party is in two days, and we have to have them in Aaron's
hands on that night."

"Listen, I understand your concern. But don't work yourself up. On the night of the party, Simon will be escorting me
there. And when I arrive, I will check in with you by intro-
ducing myself. An hour into the party, Simon is going to slip

away so he can find the evidence we need to lock those brothers up for those two murders. You will be fine. Don't shut down on me right now, okay?"

"Okay."

"All right, now if you need anything, call this office back and have them transfer your call directly to me, okay?"

"Okay," I answered.

Agent Tracy and I went over a few more things, like keeping each other company at the party after Simon snuck off. She also informed me that she would be wired up and that the other agents would be outside waiting to take everyone down when told to do so. I've gotta admit that she put me at ease. But I knew the best satisfaction wouldn't happen until Troy, Aaron, and Noah were locked away somewhere. They were all dangerous and racist men, and they needed to be behind bars.

Now I didn't know if my parents would be put in witness protection after all of this was said and done, but if they did, I would make sure that they were well taken care of. They were all I had, and I couldn't let Troy, Aaron, or Noah take them from me.

Even more important, I wouldn't let them take me from my parents.

18

Yoshi

I couldn't believe how fast the Weinsteins' annual party got here. It was held in the basement of this corporate building. I didn't know until now that the Weinsteins owned it. It's literally a historical building. When Troy picked me up in the valet station of my parents' building, the first thing I said was: "I gave them to a friend to hold for me."

"I thought you said that you put them in a safety-deposit box?"

"They were. I picked them up today and gave them to a friend of mine to hold on to."

"But that doesn't make sense."

"Look, I know the twins aren't that fond of me. They'll get their photos back, but I want them to pay me. That way, I can have some start-up money when I relocate to Florida."

"What if they don't go for it?"

"They will."

"You're putting me in a bind. I told Aaron that I would

bring them to him tonight. And now I don't have them. Do you know how that's going to make me look?" Troy pressured me.

"Tell him to give you another day."

"He's not gonna go for it."

"Just try," I insisted.

I could tell that Troy was really frustrated with me. At one point, he acted like he was going to spaz out at me. I'm just glad that he didn't.

The ride to the gala was pretty much quiet. I convinced him to play some music so that it wouldn't be that awkward. He did. Thankfully, the tension was at an all-time low.

When all of the guests arrived, we were ushered onto the elevators and taken down to the bottom floor. It was a banquet room, with a stage and side doors on each side of the room. I saw the portraits of men dating back to the 1800s. They were all members. Pioneers. And they sat upright in the portraits with Dragon symbols stitched on their suit jackets, and they wore alumni shoulder sashes with gold Mason medallions with dragons inside hanging from their necks.

All of the men looked prestigious. And there wasn't a black man in sight. But I knew that before I had a chance to look at all of the portraits. Special Agent Petty had been right, this was some serious secret-society brotherhood shit.

"Brought you a glass of champagne," Troy said as he handed the glass to me.

I hesitated for a second, afraid to drink it, knowing that everyone here was known for spiking drinks. However, when I thought about the FBI not being too far away, I relaxed a little and took a sip.

"Good, isn't it?" he asked after waiting for me to drink it.

"Yes, it's really nice."

"Want to meet some of the firm's clients?" he asked me.

"No, I'm fine right here," I insisted.

"Want something to eat? We have caviar. Truffles. We even have wild mushrooms."

"Maybe later," I told him, and then I changed the subject. "So those guys in the portraits on the wall founded this brotherhood?"

"Yes, as a matter of fact, they did. Come here, let me show you who my grandfather was," Troy insisted, and pulled me in the direction of the portraits. He pointed to a very old man with glasses. His name was Tatem Bower. The gold leaf at the bottom of the picture read that he was inducted in 1915. One portrait over was Tatem's great-grandfather, and he was inducted in 1870. This information was mind-blowing. Now I could see why it was so easy for Troy to call me racist names. His entire damn family were the KKK, if you want to be technical.

"This is awesome, huh? My grandfather and his grandfather placed right beside one another."

"Were they attorneys too?"

"Yep, they sure were."

"Why isn't your father up here?"

"Because he died before he could be inducted."

"Are you looking forward to getting your portrait up there?" I asked him. It was test time.

"Not really. See, I'm not as smart as they were. It takes a confident man to fill their shoes."

"You can be confident at times."

"Yeah, I know. But I'm nothing like them."

"Are the Weinstein brothers' fathers and grandfathers somewhere on these walls?" I changed the subject because I could tell that his bipolar disorder was about to kick in, full throttle.

"Yeah, they're over here," he replied, and pulled me to the wall opposite of where we were standing. And just like his grandfathers were positioned on the wall, so were the Weinstein men. The first portrait he pointed out was Noah and Aaron's father. "This is their father. The great Arthur Bell Weinstein. He was inducted in 1931. His father, Wilson Moore Weinstein, was inducted in 1910. And Wilson's father, Conrad Wesley Weinstein, was inducted in 1895. And next to him is Conrad's father, Tom Winchester Weinstein, who was inducted in 1863. Conrad was one of the founding fathers of this brotherhood, so the tradition must continue on," he explained.

"Thanks for the history lesson," I said.

"You're welcome," he replied.

I was being sarcastic though. I really didn't want to be here, especially after finding out that I was supposed to be a sacrificial lamb. These racist men called it a *cleansing*, but I called it a *slaughterhouse*.

Fifteen minutes later, I saw Simon coming into the room. Troy saw him the same time I did. And I could see the anger building up inside of him. I grabbed his arm and said, "Calm down. Remember, I told you that he will no longer bother me. Besides, he's got a guest with him."

Troy took a deep breath and then leaned over and started whispering, "If I see him trying to talk to you, I will have him removed from this building."

"Tonight is not the time for that. This is Aaron and Noah's annual party. Let's do away with the drama for one night. Okay?"

Troy closed his eyes and then reopened them. "I will do it for you. But after tonight, you are off limits. Deal?"

"Deal," I said, even though there wasn't going to be a tomorrow for him and me. I was getting on the first thing going out of New York, and I was not looking back for at least six months to a year. Maybe by then, I could get my parents to come visit me, instead of me visiting them.

I noticed that as Simon moved farther into the room, Noah and Aaron started paying a lot of attention to him. I didn't know if it was the woman he had on his arm, or they wanted to make sure that he didn't rattle Troy's brain by interacting with me. Either way, their eyes were glued to him.

Seeing Tracy for the first time made me do a double take. She was a very attractive woman. She kind of resembled the actress Julia Roberts. In a million years, you wouldn't think that she could be an undercover FBI agent. She was *that* beautiful and she glided across the floor effortlessly.

"I see your ex-boyfriend has a new girlfriend," Troy commented. He was trying to get a reaction out of me.

"He's not my ex-boyfriend," I refuted.

"Good answer," he replied.

"What, are you playing a game with me?" I asked him, and then I took a sip of my champagne.

"Let's not get into an argument. Remember, you said that now isn't the time for that."

"Yes, I did. But you will be dealt with appropriately if I see you smiling in his face."

Taken aback by Troy's bipolar antics, I stood there and wondered how I got caught up being in the company of this guy again. One freaking minute, he's cool, and then the next minute, he wants to talk shit to me and rip my head off. I can't deal with him and his bullshit. I swear, if tonight didn't hurry up and end, I would end it myself.

I watched as Simon made his way around the room. He shook hands with almost everyone in here. If only they knew that he was a mole planted in this circle by the FBI. I was sure a lot of these men would have his head if they knew that he was a snitch. I couldn't wait to see Aaron's and Noah's faces when they realized that the contract Simon signed was bogus. Unbeknownst to them, the ink on those documents wasn't worth a penny, and the contract wouldn't hold up in any court of law. Too bad for them.

"Let's go and get another drink," Troy insisted. And before I could answer, he looped his arm into mine and then he casually pulled me in the direction he was walking. I knew what he was doing. He didn't want to leave me alone long enough for Simon to rub elbows with mine. Troy was being a real asshole.

After he grabbed drinks for the both of us, he escorted me over to where Aaron and Noah's wives were standing. They were talking to another woman, who I assumed was their age. They were all dressed in black gowns, draped with huge pearl earrings and necklaces.

"Good evening, ladies, enjoying the festivities?" Troy greeted them. All three turned their attention toward us.

"Of course, we are," Noah's wife said. "What about you two?" she asked Troy.

"Everything is lovely," he assured her.

"You must be the new intern at the firm," Aaron's wife inquired.

I smiled. "Yes, that would be me."

"Are you two dating?" Noah's wife wanted to know.

"We're just friends," Troy interjected. It was like he had to get in front of the question.

Another woman would've been offended by his remark, I wasn't. I think the wives were shocked by my reaction.

"So no wedding bells anytime soon, huh?" Noah's wife pressed the issue.

"No. I'm too young for that. My first priority is to pass the bar exam, become a partner, and then maybe I will consider settling down and getting married. Did I mention that he must be rich too?" I answered, and chuckled. I wanted all three of these rich old ladies to know that I was special and I wasn't looking for any handouts.

"Sounds like a tough cookie, huh?" Aaron's wife commented.

"You ladies have fun," Troy stated, and then he escorted me away from them. "What was that all about?" he asked me. He acted like he had venom in his tongue.

"Nothing. I was just having a nice chat with the rich old ladies. Any harm in doing that?" I questioned him. I needed to let him know that this was a two-way street.

"Don't play games with me, Yoshi."

"Likewise," I commented. I wasn't backing down from his ass tonight.

While Troy escorted me around the room, Simon outsmarted him. He persuaded Aaron to walk him over to us to discuss the possibility of him and Troy going to the golf tournament and playing high-stakes games for money. It was pure genius on Simon's part. And FBI Agent Tracy was front and center to witness it.

"Hey, Troy, Simon was just saying that if Noah and I invite you two down to the golf tournament, he would put some serious money on the table. What do you think? Want to challenge it?" Aaron suggested.

Troy looked at Simon and then he looked at Noah. It was written all over Troy's face that he wasn't feeling this conversation or the presence of Simon. Aaron saw it too and cracked a joke. "I don't think Troy here is ready to take your money, Simon."

Simon, undercover FBI agent Tracy, and I all laughed because we thought what Aaron said was funny. To further slice the tension in half, Tracy extended her hand to Troy and me to shake, after she introduced herself to us.

"Hi there, my name is Tracy, and I am Simon's date tonight."

I shook her hand first and Troy followed suit.

"Are you enjoying yourself?" I asked while Troy eyed Simon.

"I'm not accepting any answer but yes," Aaron teased.

Tracy smiled. "Don't worry, I'm having a blast. Nice event."

"Thank you," Aaron replied.

"How often do you have these galas?" Tracy asked Aaron while Troy continued to stare in Simon's direction.

"This particular black-tie affair only happens annually," Aaron told her, and then he asked her to excuse him. Immediately thereafter, he grabbed Troy by the arm and asked him to follow him. In a flash, Troy was being dragged across the floor to the other side of the room.

While Troy was being chewed out by Aaron, this was the perfect time to get in a few words.

"I thought I would never be freed from him," I said.

"Neither did I," Simon chimed in.

"Troy really doesn't like Simon, huh?" Tracy asked.

"He was fine talking about Simon last night. But I think what happens is, when Simon is in the same room as Troy, he feels threatened about his personal space," I noted.

"No, I think it's deeper than that," Simon suggested.

"You may be right. But Troy has a bipolar condition, so he could flip the scripts on a person in one heartbeat. He is a loose cannon," I stated.

"Are we still on, as planned?" Tracy changed the subject.

"My end is covered," I replied.

"Mine too," Simon remarked.

"Are you sure you're good? I don't like the tone of your voice," Tracy told Simon.

"I just can't wait until this thing is done. I don't feel safe in this place," Simon explained.

"And how do you think I feel? My head is on the chopping block tonight," I told him.

"Now is not the time to stress out, you two. Simon, I'm going to need you to slip to the back and get into Aaron's or Noah's office. Remember, we're told that it's near the men's restroom. So, when you get inside, we need you to find something that ties them to the murders that happened a year ago. Our source says that there are memorabilia and trophies celebrating the murderers for their kill, so that's what we need," Tracy indicated.

"That is so sadistic, and the thought of that makes me sick to my stomach," I told them.

"Let's face it, we have some evil people in this world," Tracy stated.

"Hey, let's change the subject. Troy is coming in hot from the west side of you, Yoshi. Don't act nervous. Just be yourself. I will act like we were talking about you doing some charity work for the Boys and Girls Clubs," Tracy said.

"I think that is a wonderful idea," I agreed. I said it loud enough for Troy to hear it as he approached us.

"What's a wonderful idea?" he wanted to know. He wasn't missing a beat.

"Tracy has invited me to speak at the Boys and Girls Clubs sometime in the near future."

"What would you be speaking about?" he pressed me.

"It would be on our next career day," Tracy interjected. I guess she saw me scrambling to come up with a good explanation as to why I'd pay a visit to the club.

"I was talking to Yoshi," he replied sarcastically.

"Come on now, Troy, let's cut it out. You're being very disrespectful to my date," Simon got up the gumption to say. I swear, it came out of left field and I was proud.

Troy took one step toward Simon. "If you think I'm being disrespectful, then you and your guest need to leave," Troy insisted.

"Stop it, Troy. I'm so over it with your mood swings. Just yesterday you were cool and we talked about Simon with no arguments, and now you're busting his balls. What's your deal?" I got up the courage to say.

"These last few days, I just don't like how much time you two been spending together," Troy finally fessed up.

"But you know what that was for," I added, trying to defuse this situation.

"You know Noah and Aaron are using all of their resources to find out who stole the photos?" Troy confessed.

"Is that why you've been hot one minute and cold the next?" I asked him.

"I don't want to talk about that right now. She could be working with them." Troy flipped the script again.

"I can walk away," Tracy offered.

"No, it's too late. You've heard enough already," Troy stated, and then he grabbed my arm and said, "Come on, let's get out of here."

I resisted his tug. "Where are we going?" I asked.

"We're getting out of here. Aaron and Noah have been acting really weird. And I don't like the way they've been looking at you and me."

"So we're leaving the party, just like that?" I wondered aloud.

"Yes, we are," he said, and then yanked on my arm.

I stood there firmly, refusing to move. "Let go of my arm, Troy."

But he wasn't giving up. He was adamant about leaving the event and taking me with him. "I'm doing this for your own good," he warned me.

I could see in his eyes that he knew the time was drawing near, and before the night was over, he would be forced to murder me as a sacrificial lamb.

"But I'm not ready to go," I informed him, also knowing what tonight would bring, but I knew I was protected and that the FBI was standing right outside of these doors. Nothing was going to happen to me.

"I'm not going to say it again," he threatened, and yanked

my arm really hard. Half of the guests in the room saw it.
Noah and Aaron included. And it infuriated them so much
that Aaron stormed toward us. Noah followed in Aaron's
footsteps.

"What is your problem? And release her arm at this very
moment. You are embarrassing us in front of all of our guests,"
Aaron growled at Troy.

Troy released my arm. "I'm trying to take her outside so
we can talk about how it would benefit everyone at the firm
that we get along," he lied.

I wanted to tell Aaron and Noah both that he was lying,
but I knew I'd blow our cover tonight if I did. Troy was going
through one of his spells, so I had to treat him with kid
gloves right now.

"Yoshi, is that true?" Aaron asked me.

I hesitated, and then I lied and covered Troy's ass. "Yes, it's
true."

"Well, in that case, that's fine. But it's not a good thing to
do it in front of guests," Noah chimed in.

"I'm sorry. And I apologize," Troy told him.

"Don't let it happen again," Aaron warned him.

"I won't," Troy assured them.

As soon as Aaron and Noah stepped away, Troy started
whispering threats at me. This fucking guy was off his
rocker!

"See, it's your fault that they came over here to embarrass
me in front of everyone. If you would've just listened to me
and left with me when I told you, none of this would've happened. So now I'm gonna have to get rid of you," he hissed in
my ear.

I swear, Troy was a modern-day Dr. Jekyll and Mr. Hyde.

Instantly fear-stricken, I stood there in awe. I didn't know
what to say to this guy. But then it came to me: "Get rid of
me. What does that mean?"

He smiled and said, "You'll see."

Now I was paralyzed. From my neck down, I couldn't move. The mess that had come from his mouth tonight left me believing that Troy hadn't taken his meds in a few days, at least. For him to stand there and tell me that I should trust him and leave with him, and then to say that he was going to get rid of me, spooked me. At this point, nothing would make me feel better than for the FBI to crash this place right now and take everyone involved with this madness into custody.

Tracy must've seen that my mood had changed and decided that she wanted to come over and perhaps do some damage control.

"I forgot to ask you," she started off saying after getting within arm's reach of Troy and me, "can I get your phone number so that I can call you later on in the week?"

"Sure, do you have something to write with?" I asked her, and was relieved at the same time that she walked over to check up on me.

She reached down into her clutch bag and pulled out a pen and a handheld personal phone book, while Troy stood next to us both. He didn't blink an eye. While I was giving her my home telephone number, Aaron stepped up to our circle and asked Troy to follow him.

"Come with me, I want you to meet someone," he told him. Troy had no choice but to leave with Aaron, and I could see that he was not happy about it.

"Thank God! We can breathe for a few minutes," I commented.

"Don't look back."

"What's going on?"

"He's looking back at us. So I'm going to pretend that I'm writing down your number," Tracy declared. "While I'm standing here, I might as well tell you that Simon left the room."

"Oh my God, he's gone. It's happening already?" I asked her. At one point, it felt like I was about to hyperventilate. Tracy saw it too.

"Calm down and breathe," she coached me.

"Is Troy still looking in our direction?" I wondered aloud.

"Not now. He's talking to Aaron, Noah, and another gentleman," she answered me. "You're doing good. Just slow down a little more," she continued to coach me.

I took a couple of deep breaths and then I exhaled. "Is he looking over here now?" I asked her once again.

"No, he's still engaged in the conversation with those men," she reassured me.

"What about Simon? Think he's all right?"

"Yes, he's fine. He got one of the hosts to show him where the men's restroom was. I'm communicating with Special Agent Petty through my ear device now."

"How long has he been back there?"

"Three minutes, if that," Tracy informed me. "Oh shit! Troy and Aaron are walking toward the side door where his office is located," Tracy added.

Without hesitation, I turned slightly and looked over my shoulders and confirmed what Tracy had just told me. Troy and Aaron were leaving the room, and this could be bad.

"What should we do?" I asked her.

"Petty, I think we may have a problem," Tracy said.

I couldn't see the device she was speaking through, and it didn't matter. The only thing that mattered was that we had muscle from the feds not too far away.

"He knows that they are coming," she whispered to me.

"Is he in the restroom or the office?" I probed her.

"Petty, is he in the office yet?" Tracy spoke through the mic, and then she fell silent.

"What are they saying?" I wanted to know.

"Petty is saying that he can't hear anything. He's quiet," Tracy answered, then fell silent again.

I stood there numb. Paralyzed. Not knowing what was about to happen next.

"If you want me to go back there, just say the word," Tracy added as she talked into the mic near her ear. But no order was given, so she and I stood there like sitting ducks.

19
Troy

Aaron said it was time to prep me for tonight's cleansing, so he had to pull me from the event. "Let's go to my office and get you ready," he said.

While he led me away from the crowded festivities, I looked back at Yoshi to see what she was doing. Simon was nowhere in sight, but that didn't matter to me. I hated when I saw Yoshi interacting with other people. In my mind, it felt like they were stealing time from me. No one understood my love-hate relationship with her. In reality, she and I won't ever live happily ever after, so it would be in my best interest to get rid of her. That way, no one else would have her.

"Where is it going to happen?" I asked after we entered his office.

He flipped the light switch on and then closed the door behind us. He and I were alone.

"Have a seat," he instructed me.

I sat down and admired the portraits and awards that

adorned his wall. "You won all of those awards?" I wanted
to know.

Aaron stood before me proudly. "Yes, as a matter of fact, I
did," he responded as he pulled two sets of black leather
gloves from a safe hiding behind one of the portraits. He
grabbed a nine-millimeter next. At the end of the barrel was
a silencer. "Put on these gloves," he said after he tossed the
gloves across his desk.

As instructed, I slipped on the leather gloves. "This will
prevent me from getting the gun powder from the bullets,
right?"

"Smart guy." He smiled at me.

"So we're about to do it now?" I said anxiously.

"Yes, we're about to do it now," he agreed, and then he
pulled back on the chamber, pointing the barrel at me.
"Where are the photos of Simon and Yoshi?"

Alarmed by Aaron's change of heart, I stood up from my
chair and raised both of my hands. "Wait, what are you
doing?" I questioned him.

"Answer me," Aaron demanded as he took a step toward me.

"I don't have them. I told you that Yoshi took them," I
told him, my heart racing at an uncontrollable speed. I could
not believe that Aaron was pointing his gun at me.

"You're a fucking liar. I've got you on camera," he told me.

"Which camera is that? There are no cameras in your office," I refuted.

"Answer my question, Troy. Where are the photos? I
know you have them." Aaron wouldn't let up. He was deter-
mined to get that information out of me. But I couldn't tell
him that I took the photos from his office. He'd kill me for
sure then.

"I don't have those photos."

"I'm only going to ask you one more time."

"Yoshi has them. I told you that she went into your office
and stole them."

"Never mind all of that. I told you to have them in my hands tonight, didn't I?" he reminded me, and took another step toward me.

"I can go and get them from her now. Just give me a chance to make it right," I insisted. But in reality, I didn't have the photos. Yoshi didn't have them with her either.

"You know what, Troy? You're weak and you're a liability. You aren't taking your meds, and you're making Noah and me look bad."

"So you're gonna kill me?"

"Noah and I have gone back and forth about how to deal with you. We know that you stole the photos from my office and gave them to Yoshi. This last stunt you pulled, and wanting to continue a relationship with her even after we told you to separate yourself from her, was the last straw for us. You're a wild card, Troy, and we feel that this is the best course of action for all parties involved."

"But I thought that you were about to prep me to cleanse my soul and rid the universe of trash like Yoshi. You said that I would be doing the world a favor. Killing all of the non-white people, immigrants, and homosexuals was the way. You told me this."

"Yes, I did. Because that is our way, but you've been brainwashed. Somehow you have become obsessed with that nigga girl and you can't leave her alone or get her out of your head. Now tell me why is that?"

"I can change," I told him. But, thinking about it, I knew it was impossible. He was right. I was obsessed with Yoshi. There was no way that I would be able to allow her to walk around in the city with a new suitor, since it was not socially acceptable for her and me to be together. And if I allowed Aaron to kill me now, I would lose all my power and go to hell without Yoshi, and I couldn't let that happen.

Without giving it any more thought, I rushed toward Aaron, simultaneously eyeing the nine-millimeter handgun he had pointed directly at me. But before I could get my hands on him, I collapsed onto the floor. At that very moment, I knew that I had been shot. And when I looked up at Aaron, he was standing over me, with the gun clutched firmly in his hand.

"I told Noah that we should've done this a long time ago," he said, and then he released another shot. After that, everything around me went dark.

20
Yoshi

Tracy and I stood there in limbo trying to determine whether or not she should check on Simon. But Special Agent Petty insisted that she stand down. I had a lot of questions, and so did Agent Tracy, but no one was giving either of us any answers. Then a few minutes later, the same side door that Aaron and Troy slipped behind opened up and Aaron peered out of it. He got Noah's attention and signaled him to join him. Without hesitation, Noah left the floor and joined Aaron. The side door closed immediately thereafter.

"What is going on?" I asked Agent Tracy.

"I don't know." Then she talked into her mic device. "Aaron just opened the side door and summoned Noah to come with him." I couldn't hear what Petty was saying, but when Tracy displayed an expression of frustration, I knew that he hadn't changed his mind about her standing down.

The side door opened again, but no one appeared. All you could see was another wall from where we were standing.

"The door just opened, but no one is there," I mentioned.

Agent Tracy relayed that bit of information to Special Agent Petty through the device. But once again, she was told not to move.

Growing more and more frustrated, I said, "I will go back there if you want me to." But five seconds after volunteering to check things out, the side door closed.

"The side door just closed," she said into the device.

"Now I'm getting worried," I acknowledged.

So many things started running through my mind, and I couldn't come up with a plausible answer as to what was going on. While Agent Tracy continued to brief Special Agent Petty through her listening device, I became a nervous wreck, wondering where Simon and Troy were, and why Aaron flagged Noah to join him behind that side door.

Then two more minutes passed and the side door opened again. This time, Noah peered out from behind the door and flagged me to come to him.

"Oh my God! Do you see this?" I started off saying after realizing what Noah was doing.

"Is he motioning you to come to him?" Tracy asked me.

"Yes, he is. What should I do?" I asked her. My stomach was bottled up in a bottomless pit of nerves.

"If you don't go, he's gonna think something is wrong," Agent Tracy advised me.

"But what if I don't come back out?" I noted.

"Noah is standing at the side door, motioning for Yoshi to come to him," Agent Tracy reported into the device.

"Oh my God! He's walking toward me," I told her. My freaking heart was about to jump out of my chest.

"Petty, Noah is walking toward us right now. What should we do?" Tracy continued to brief Agent Petty through her mic.

"He's still coming," I informed her, pretending to look in another direction. I had my peripheral vision working overtime.

"Hey, Yoshi, do you mind coming with me?" Noah asked as he nudged me in my left arm.

I turned around and faced him as if I were shocked to see him. "What's going on?" I replied, acting as clueless as I possibly could.

"Just come with me," he said flatly.

"Can you tell me where the women's restroom is?" Agent Tracy inquired.

"Yes, where is it? I've gotta go to the little girls' bathroom too," I chimed in. I knew that I needed to do everything within my power to prolong going with Noah alone behind that door. In my mind, Troy was back there with Aaron, and the only reason why Noah wanted me to join them was because they wanted me to answer for the photos that Troy stole from Aaron's office, nearly a week ago. It wouldn't surprise me to know Troy was throwing all of the blame on me.

"The ladies' room is in the back. I can escort you both back there," he said eagerly.

Relieved that I wasn't going to be with Noah and the other guys alone, I exhaled and followed Tracy and Noah to the partially opened door.

As we approached it, it opened and out came Simon, running. He was able to drag Troy to the doorway. "Troy has been shot! Aaron shot him and he's dying!" he shouted. He was heavily winded.

Startled, I stopped in my tracks. "Arrest Noah! He shot and killed Aaron," Simon added as he hurled strong allegations about Noah's involvement.

Immediately after Simon made these accusations, Noah took off running in the opposite direction. He didn't get too far, because Agent Tracy shot off in his direction and tackled him, ending in a scuffle with him falling down on the floor. Everyone in attendance stood by in awe.

"Get off me, you fucking bitch!" Noah roared. He was angry that Agent Tracy had him pinned down on the floor.

I bolted toward Troy as he lay in the entryway of the door. Simon moved to the side so that I could get down on the floor and cradle Troy in my arms. He blinked his eyes while gurgling the blood in his mouth. I discouraged him from talking, but he wouldn't listen to me.

"Aaron wanted the photos and shot me when I didn't give them to him," he said. "Noah killed Aaron. Noah said that he was tired of Aaron bringing attention to the firm. He said that Aaron was tearing down everything that Noah built, so he had to stop him because he wasn't going down with him." Troy paused then, like he was thinking of something else to say.

I rocked him back and forth while shedding a few tears.

"I'm sorry for the way I've been treating you."

I told him that I accepted his apology, and while I was with Troy, I glanced over at Agent Tracy, who by now had lifted Noah up from the floor and placed handcuffs on him.

"You better have probable cause for arresting me, because I will have your job at the peak of dawn," Noah threatened her.

"Let's talk about the two men you had murdered in one of your sacrificial cleansing ceremonies," I heard Agent Tracy ask him.

"*Murdered*? I don't know what you're talking about, young lady. Do you know that you are completely out of line?" Noah continued to gripe. He was both angry and humiliated that he was standing in the middle of the floor of his annual gala handcuffed in front of all his guests. Everyone was standing in huddles, whispering to one another.

"Maybe I am, but you are going to jail tonight," Agent Tracy announced to him.

"You are not taking me anywhere," he spat out. Within minutes of this fiasco, twelve FBI agents walked through the front door and had the place surrounded. Special Agent Petty was front and center. Arrests were being made throughout the room. Five of the firm's senior partners were taken out in handcuffs. Noah was taken out next.

By then, Troy had passed away in my arms. Here I was, losing someone else to death. If I had gone with Noah, would I be lying here? Why was I always escaping death? Was I next?

I knew one thing for sure. When I started the next chapter of my life, things were going to be different. It was time to take charge of my life. No matter what.

See how it all started in

PLAYING WITH FIRE

And catch up with where Yoshi Lomax is now, with

PLAYING DIRTY

And

NOTORIOUS

Available now

From Dafina Books

Wherever books are sold